The

I am a vampire. For centuries I believed I was the last vampire on Earth, that I was the most powerful creature in existence. That belief gave me great self-confidence. I feared nothing because nothing could harm me. Then one remarkable day, my supposedly dead creator, Yaksha, came for me, and I discovered I was not omnipotent. A short time later another vampire appeared, one Eddie Fender. He had Yaksha's strength, and once again I was almost destroyed. Yet I survived both Yaksha and Eddie, only to give birth to a daughter of unfathomable power and incomprehensible persuasion—Kalika, Kali Ma, the Dark Mother, the Supreme Goddess of Destruction. Yes, I believe my only child to be a divine incarnation, an *avatar,* as some would describe her. In a devastating vision she showed me her infinite greatness. The only problem is that my daughter seems to have been born without a conscience.

Actually, I do have three other small problems.

I don't know where Kalika is.

I know I must destroy her.

And I love her.

Books by Christopher Pike

BURY ME DEEP
CHAIN LETTER 2: THE ANCIENT EVIL
DIE SOFTLY
THE ETERNAL ENEMY
FALL INTO DARKNESS
FINAL FRIENDS #1: THE PARTY
FINAL FRIENDS #2: THE DANCE
FINAL FRIENDS #3: THE GRADUATION
GIMME A KISS
THE IMMORTAL
LAST ACT
THE LAST VAMPIRE
THE LAST VAMPIRE 2: BLACK BLOOD
THE LAST VAMPIRE 3: RED DICE
THE LAST VAMPIRE 4: PHANTOM
THE LAST VAMPIRE 5: EVIL THIRST
THE LOST MIND
MASTER OF MURDER
THE MIDNIGHT CLUB
MONSTER
REMEMBER ME
REMEMBER ME 2: THE RETURN
REMEMBER ME 3: THE LAST STORY
ROAD TO NOWHERE
SCAVENGER HUNT
SEE YOU LATER
SPELLBOUND
THE STARLIGHT CRYSTAL
THE VISITOR
WHISPER OF DEATH
THE WICKED HEART
WITCH

Available from ARCHWAY Paperbacks

Christopher Pike

The Last Vampire 5
EVIL THIRST

AN ARCHWAY PAPERBACK
Published by POCKET BOOKS
New York London Toronto Sydney Tokyo Singapore

This book is a work of fiction. Names, characters, places and incidents are products of the author's imagination or are used fictitiously. Any resemblance to actual events or locales or persons, living or dead, is entirely coincidental.

AN ARCHWAY PAPERBACK *Original*

An Archway Paperback published by
POCKET BOOKS, a division of Simon & Schuster Inc.
1230 Avenue of the Americas, New York, NY 10020

ISBN: 0-671-55050-0

First Archway Paperback printing July 1996

10 9 8 7 6 5 4 3 2 1

AN ARCHWAY PAPERBACK and colophon are registered trademarks of Simon & Schuster Inc.

Cover art by Joe Danisi

Printed in the U.S.A.

IL 9+

For my sister Ann, who is a vampire

The Last Vampire 5
EVIL THIRST

I am a vampire. For centuries I believed I was the last vampire on Earth, that I was the most powerful creature in existence. That belief gave me great self-confidence. I feared nothing because nothing could harm me. Then one remarkable day, my supposedly dead creator, Yaksha, came for me, and I discovered I was not omnipotent. A short time later another vampire appeared, one Eddie Fender. He had Yaksha's strength, and once again I was almost destroyed. Yet I survived both Yaksha and Eddie, only to give birth to a daughter of unfathomable power and incomprehensible persuasion— Kalika, Kali Ma, the Dark Mother, the Supreme Goddess of Destruction. Yes, I believe my only child to be a divine incarnation, an *avatar,* as some would describe her. In a devastating vision she showed me her infinite greatness. The only problem is that my daughter seems to have been born without a conscience.

Actually, I do have three other small problems.

I don't know where Kalika is.

I know I must destroy her.

And I love her.

I don't know which of these dilemmas is worst, but together they make a very dangerous combination. There is another child who has recently been born to rival my daughter. I don't know the child's first name, but he is the son of my friend, Paula Ramirez. The power of this child is still a mystery to me. I only know that a tiny vial of his blood was able to bring my closest friend, Seymour Dorsten, back from the dead. I don't know where Paula and her son are either. I don't know if they're with Kalika. If they are, I do know they are both probably dead. Above all else, my daughter wants this child.

But why? I don't know.

I am beset with problems.

They seem never to stop.

I stand outside the Unity Church in Santa Monica, Seymour Dorsten by my side. Three months have passed since we were last in Santa Monica, on the pier. On that day Kalika first chose to spare Seymour's life, but then threw a stake into his spine while he thrashed in the ocean water below us. She said she did so to make a point.

"Do you really need to know?"

"Yes."

"The knowledge will cost you."

The question I had asked was who Paula's child was. Killing Seymour was her answer to the question, a very curious answer. Had Kalika not killed Seymour, I never would have thought to use the child's blood on a dead person. I never would have known just how special the child was. Yet Seymour does not remember any of this. The shock of being impaled has dimmed his memory of that night's events. He remembers being thrown off the pier and into the water—that's it. Of course he is still pressuring me to make him a vampire. He thinks then we will have great sex, or at least *some* sex. I don't sleep with him because I am afraid it would destroy our delicate balance of love and insults.

For the tenth time Seymour wants to know why I have dragged him to a New Age lecture. It is entitled: The Birth of Christ—an Egyptian Prophecy Fulfilled. The speaker is to be a Dr. Donald Seter, founder of the New Age group, the Suzama Society. I want to attend Dr. Seter's talk because of two incredible facts he has publicly announced. On a radio talk show he stated that Christ has been reborn—his birth took place on the exact day Paula's child was born. Of course he makes no mention of Paula and does not know to whom the child was born. The second fact is his claim that he has in his possession an ancient Egyptian scripture that supposedly gives details of this rebirth.

I would immediately discount the latter claim if the date had not been so personally coincidental, and if I had not happened to have known the original Suzama when I was in Egypt almost five thousand years ago. At one point Suzama was my teacher, and I know for a fact she was clairvoyant.

Yet I have never heard of the Suzama scripture before.

I wonder where Dr. Seter obtained it, and how accurate it is.

But these things I can't explain to Seymour without telling him that he was brought back to life by the blood of a three-hour-old Hispanic infant. I feel there is a reason for his memory block, and I hesitate to tamper with it. Besides, I am afraid he might not believe me if I told him the truth. Who would? It is difficult to contemplate God and His Son and immaculate conceptions without feeling like a potential fanatic. Especially since Paula was not—in her own words—a virgin.

"We could be at a movie," Seymour says. "We could be having dinner. Besides, this whole Christian thing bores me. They have been waiting two thousand years for him to show up. If he was coming back, he would be here already."

"Krishna promised to return," I say. "He said he would not be recognized."

"He won't be bringing his flute?"

"I think he will return in humble surroundings."

Seymour studies the poster outside the church announcing the lecture. "You *are* history. What can you learn from this joker?"

I have to let something slip or Seymour won't attend. Actually, I'm not sure why I've brought him, but I suppose I know that at some point I'll have to open my heart to him and ask his advice. I always have in the past. I want him at the lecture so that he'll have all the facts when I need his advice.

Yet I hesitate before speaking. Every time I bring him deeper into my life, I bring him closer to danger. Still, I remind myself, it is his decision to stay with me, even after he has seen what my daughter can do. He at least knows that I am searching for her, even if he doesn't realize I am also desperately seeking Paula and her child. Yet Paula hasn't called the number I gave her to call. She should have tried to contact me two months ago, a month after I said good-bye to her. It worries me that Kalika may have gotten to her first. I am at Dr. Seter's lecture in the hope that he can give me some clue as to where they might be. It is unlikely, I know.

"Dr. Seter says he has a copy of a scripture Suzama wrote," I tell Seymour. "She was a real person, a revered priestess of the Church of Isis, a high adept in ancient Egypt." I pause. "I knew her, I studied with her."

Seymour is impressed. "What did she teach you?"

"How to bring the white light above my head into my heart."

"What?"

"She taught primarily esoteric forms of meditation. She had many gifts." I grab his arm and drag him toward the church door. "I will tell you more about her later."

On the way in there is a registration table and a donation basket. I throw a few dollars in the latter. A young man in a dark blue suit and a red tie stands near the door greeting people. Actually, there are a number of people similarly outfitted—young, handsome people, males and females, wearing navy blue clothes and shiny faces. They are Dr. Seter's followers, I realize, but I hesitate to make the judgment that the man has formed a cult. Not all New Age groups, or Christian groups for that matter, signify sects. Besides, I don't care if he has formed a cult or not. I just care if he knows what he's talking about.

The young man greeting people pauses to say hello to me.

"Welcome," he says. "May I ask how you heard about our lecture?"

"On the radio," I say. "Yesterday night. I heard Dr. Seter's interview."

"KEXT?" he asks.

"That was the one," I say. "Have you known the doctor long?"

"I should say." The young man smiles and offers his hand. "James Seter—I work for my father. Have since I can remember." He pauses. "And your name?"

"I'm Alisa. This is Seymour."

"Hi," Seymour says, shaking James's hand when I'm through with it. But James Seter only has eyes for me.

"Have you read Dr. Seter's book?" he asks me.

"No," I say. "I was hoping to obtain a copy here."

"They will be on sale after the lecture," James says. "Fascinating reading, if I do say so myself."

"What allowed your father to predict so accurately the birth of Christ?" I ask.

"The Suzama scripture. It contains very detailed knowledge about the next coming of the messiah. It predicted Christ's coming the first time very accurately."

I smile. "And you believe all this?"

He nods. "Suzama had a great gift. Studying her words, I have never found her to make a mistake."

"It sounds like a remarkable document," I say. "Why haven't modern archeologists, linguists, and theologians had a chance to study it?"

James hesitates. "My father will address all these questions in the lecture. Better to ask him. His knowledge of the scripture is extremely comprehensive."

"Just one last question," I say. "Has he brought the original scripture with him tonight?"

"I'm afraid not. It's a priceless artifact. We cannot risk it at a public lecture."

I detect no deceit in his words, and I have a sharp ear for it. Also, there is an ease in his manner, a naturalness. He does not act like a fanatic. His dark eyes continue to study me, though. I think he likes me. He is remarkably handsome, and cannot be more than twenty-two years old.

After muttering my thanks and taking Seymour's hand, I step into the church and search for a seat. The place is crowded but we manage to squeeze in near the front. The audience is remarkably diverse, made up of old and young, tramps and professionals. I am disappointed I will not have a chance to study the scripture. I am certain I would know if it were authentic. Suzama had a fine hand for hieroglyphs. I remember her work well.

Dr. Seter enters five minutes later.

He is a small man with white hair and an unassuming manner. As he walks toward the podium, I estimate his age at seventy, although he appears less than sixty. It is his vitality and bright gray eyes that make him seem younger than he really is. He wears a medium-priced gray suit and expensive black shoes. He is not so handsome as his son, though. Indeed, I suspect he is not the biological father, that James is adopted. There is a scholarly air to Dr. Seter that I find interesting. The lines on and the planes across his face show intelligence and extensive education. I see all this in one penetrating vampiric glance.

James Seter comes forward to introduce his father. He lists a number of academic achievements. Dr. Seter has Ph.Ds in both theology and archeology, from Harvard and Stanford respectively. He is the author of numerous published papers and three books. For the last decade, James says, his father has been studying the Suzama scripture and bringing the knowledge contained in it to the world. James does not mention where his father obtained the scripture, probably to leave his father something of interest to discuss. The introduction is brief, and soon Dr. Seter is at the podium. His voice is pleasant, although somewhat reedy. He starts by welcoming us and thanking us for coming. Then he pauses and flashes a warm but shy smile.

"It is quite a claim for one to make," he says, "that one knows that the messiah is in the world. That he has been born on such and such a day in such and such a country. Had I attended this lecture as an observer ten years ago, I don't think I would have sat through the introduction. For as my son James has pointed out, I come from a fairly rigorous academic background. Until ten years ago, I never thought of the second coming or even, quite frankly, much of Christ himself. This may come as a surprise, since I hold a doctorate in theology. But the truth of the matter is my studies of religion were purely academic. I was an agnostic. I neither believed nor disbelieved the world's religions, yet I found them fascinating.

"Now this is where I may lose half of you. In fact, when I first began to lecture on the Suzama scripture, it was normal for a quarter of my audience to get up and leave at this point—my introduction to the scripture. Since those days I have managed to decrease that number by initially asking all of you to please set aside your doubts for the next few minutes to listen to what I have to say. You can form your judgments later. There is plenty of time, believe me."

Dr. Seter paused to sip from the glass of water on the podium. Then he cleared his throat and continued.

"The Suzama scripture comes from the culture of ancient Egypt. Carbon dating and an analysis of its hieroglyphic style place it back approximately five thousand years, in what is commonly called pre-dynastic Egypt. I did not find the scripture in

9

Egypt, but in a country in Western Europe that I cannot reveal at this time. The reason for this secrecy may be obvious to some, and despicable to others." He pauses. "I took the Suzama scripture back with me to America to study, without the permission of the country where I found it. In that sense I am guilty of stealing, but I make no apologies. Furthermore, as long as I refuse to name the country from which I took it, I cannot be legally prosecuted for the act. But with my background, I felt I was best equipped to study the scripture.

"Now many of you may feel that is the height of egotism on my part. By keeping the original scripture to myself I immediately bring into question its authenticity. What reputable scientist would do such a thing? If you had told me ten years ago that I would be guilty of this behavior, I would have said it would not be possible. I would have said that every ancient artifact belongs to the world. Nothing should be hidden away and kept secret. That is a basic scientific credo. And yet I have hidden this document. Why?

"Because I believe the Suzama scripture contains information that could be dangerous if publicly revealed. Dangerous to whom, you might ask? To the Christ himself, as an infant, and to the public as a whole. For Suzama, a powerful clairvoyant of her time, has set down information that might allow one to find the Christ before his time. Also, the scripture contains information on powerful forms of meditation that are, in my estimate, dangerous for the inexperienced.

"Who am I to decide what knowledge is too

dangerous for mankind to receive? I can only say in my defense that I have experimented personally with many of Suzama's instructions, and almost lost my life in the process. From my point of view, it would be the ultimate in irresponsibility to throw all of the Suzama material out there.

"Then why should you believe anything I have to say? Why should you even believe there was a Suzama? Well, you don't have to believe me. I don't ask that you do. But as a measure of proof I have turned over numerous slides of the original scripture to eminent archeologists. Because I have not allowed them access to the original artifact, they are unwilling to state unequivocally that the Suzama scripture is authentic. But many of them are willing to certify that as far as they can tell it is the real thing. A list of these experts is recorded in my book.

"What does this long dead woman have to say about the birth and rebirth of the Christ? For one thing Suzama states that Christ has not come just once, but at least four times in our history: as Lord Krishna of India, two hundred years before Suzama's birth, as Adi Shankara of India, five hundred years before Christ's birth, and finally as Christ himself. The Suzama scripture predicts each of these births, and says that the soul of all these great prophets and masters was identical. Furthermore the text predicts that this same infinite soul took birth in a human body recently, in the last three months. The exact date is given, in fact, as last March fifteenth, and the child was destined to be born here, in California."

A loud stir went through the audience. Dr. Seter pauses to have another drink of water. He deserves one, I thought, after the mouthful he had just said. Clearing his throat once more, he continues.

"What proof do I have that Suzama knew what she was talking about? If I accept her scripture as authentic, a product of ancient Egypt, then I am forced to accept that she has had a pretty good track record so far. But beyond that is the inner validation the material has given me. Following her prescribed instructions, I have been given an intuitive insight into the hidden meaning behind certain of her verses. Now I see many eyebrows rise with that statement. Are her instructions and her predictions presented in an obscure form? So obscure a form that their meaning is open to interpretation?

"The answer to both these questions is yes and no. Suzama is often specific when it comes to dates. She says when Shankara and Christ were to be born. But as far as esoteric practices are concerned she can be very subtle. A study of her text requires a study of one's own mind, and it is this last point more than any that has stopped me from letting the whole of the scripture become public. Scientists demand that knowledge be objective, empirical, when the very nature of this type of study, the search for the soul, for the God, is in my mind almost entirely a subjective exploration."

Dr. Seter pauses and scans the room. "I never like to lecture too long without taking questions. I will take some now."

Many hands shoot up. Dr. Seter chooses a

middle-aged man not far from where we are seated. The man stands to speak.

"How did you manage to find this religious text in the first place?" he asks. "What led you to it?"

Dr. Seter does not hesitate. "A dream. I simply dreamed where it was and I went and dug in a certain spot and found it."

The man is stunned. "You're not serious?"

Dr. Seter holds up his hand as a murmur goes through the crowd. "Believe me I would like to give another answer. Unfortunately another answer would not be true. This is how I found the scripture. There was no research involved, no tedious digs lasting decades. I found it as soon as I started looking for it."

The man continues to stand. "So you believe God directed you to it?"

"I believe somebody directed me to it. I don't know if it was God himself. Actually, Suzama never speaks of Christ or Shankara as God. She calls them masters, or perfected beings. And she believes we are all evolving to the same heightened state of perfection." Dr. Seter pauses. "It was an especially vivid dream, unlike any I had ever had before. It would have had to be for me to act on it, I assure you." A pause. "Next question."

He chooses a young woman at the back. Even before she speaks, it is clear she has a chip on her shoulder.

"What if I were to say that you made this all up? That the Suzama scripture is a complete fraud?"

"I would say that's not a question." Dr. Seter pauses. "Do you have a question?"

The young woman fumes. "There was only one Christ. How can you dare to compare him to these heathens?"

Dr. Seter smiles. "It is questions like this that reaffirm my decision not to make public everything I know about the Christ's birth in our time. Each of the others I spoke of was a great spiritual leader in his time. Had you been born in India, even today, you might follow their teachings. It is largely because you were born in this country that you are a Christian." He pauses. "Don't you agree?"

The young woman is uncomfortable but remains defiant. "I hardly think so. You twist the teachings of Christ, comparing them to these others."

"Frankly, I think I compliment all of them by comparing each to the other. But that is beside the point. I never asked you to believe that the Suzama scripture is accurate. I am merely saying that I believe it is, based on my research and personal experience. If you believe it is a fraud, fine. But the text warns that those who profess to worship the Christ will be the first to dismiss him when he returns."

I approve of the manner in which Dr. Seter deals with the young woman's insolent attitude. I have never appreciated religious dogma. It seems to me only a more insidious form of racial prejudice. Yet I am not sure if I agree with Dr. Seter when he says the three spiritual leaders were one and the same being. Having known Krishna personally, I have trouble reconciling many of Christ's teachings with Krishna's, although I suspect the early disciples of Christ distorted what their master said. At the same time I am familiar with Shankara's work, particularly his commentary on the Brahma Sutras, which I have studied over the centuries. I agree with the Eastern claim that Shankara was the greatest intellect who ever lived. Yet his style of teaching was very different from either Krishna's or Christ's. For one thing, he never claimed to be anyone special, either the son of God or God himself. Yet he worked many recorded miracles.

Nevertheless I find the doctor's words fascinating. I raise my hand and catch his eye, using a fraction of the great power I have in my eyes to rivet a person's attention. He immediately picks me. I also stand as I ask my question.

"You say Suzama gives exact dates as to the births of these various avatars," I say. "Yet the solar calendar was not used in ancient Egypt until two thousand B.C. Suzama surely must have used a lunar calendar when presenting her dates. How did you translate one to the other?"

"No translation was necessary. The dates are not expressed in terms of a lunar calendar but a solar one."

I am disappointed in his answer. "But you realize as an archeologist how unlikely that is. It almost certainly means the scripture you have found is either from a much later period, or that it is fake."

Dr. Seter is not dissuaded. "As an archeologist I was *surprised* she predicted the birth of these masters in terms of a solar calendar and not a lunar one. Yet if we accept as true her profound intuition, then we must also accept that she would understand that in the future her lunar calendar would not be used. Actually, at least to my mind, the fact that she did not use a lunar calendar supports her claims."

"Did she mention any other avatars besides the three you mentioned?" I ask.

Dr. Seter hesitates. "Yes. But she says they are of a different line."

"Does she mention Isis for example?"

Dr. Seter is taken aback. "I did not discuss that in any of my books. But, yes, it is true, Suzama was a high priestess of a group that worshipped Isis." He pauses. "May I ask why you ask that question?"

"We can talk about it another time," I say and quickly sit down. Seymour leans over and speaks in my ear.

"You're drawing attention to yourself," he warns.

"Only enough to make him want to meet me afterward," I reply.

"Do you think he's telling the truth?"

"He is definitely *convinced* he is telling the truth. There is not a shred of deceit in him." I pause. "But that is not the same as saying he is right. Far from it."

There followed dozens of questions.

"How did Suzama describe California?"

Answer: "At the other end of the great continent across the ocean, where the sun always shines."

"What kind of family was Christ reborn into?"

Answer: "A poor broken family."

"What nationality will the Christ be?"

Answer: "Brown skinned."

A lot of people didn't like that answer. Of course it would have made me chuckle, except Paula's baby had brown skin, like his mother.

Toward the end there was one question that disturbed me, or rather, Dr. Seter's answer did. He was asked if the reborn Christ was in any danger, as an infant. Dr. Seter hesitated long before responding. Clearly the Suzama text contained a warning of some kind.

"Yes," he says finally. "Suzama states that the forces of darkness will bend even the will of the righteous to try to find the child and destroy him. She further states that it is the duty of the old and powerful to help locate the child and protect him."

My hand is up in an instant.

"Does Suzama describe the form these forces of darkness will take?" I ask.

He pauses. "No. Not really."

It is the first lie he has told all night. Curious.

The old and powerful?

Who on the planet is older and more powerful than I am?

2

It is my desire to have coffee with Dr. Donald Seter this very night, and to increase my chances of success I send Seymour away. He's only too happy to try to catch a late movie in Westwood. Seymour, I feel, may hold me back because I plan to reach the esteemed doctor through the son, James Seter. Picking up a copy of Dr. Seter's book, *The Secret of Suzama,* on the back table for a mere twenty bucks, I stroll over to where bright-faced James is saying good-bye to people. He stands near the exit and thanks people for coming. Such a nice young man, with a firm handshake, no less. He lights up when he sees me.

"Alisa," he says. "Your questions were very interesting."

"You remember my name. I am flattered." I pause. "I am perhaps a little older than I look, and a little more educated. I have made a thorough study of ancient Egypt, and would enjoy chatting with you and your father about the Suzama scripture."

He doesn't take me seriously. "I'm sure that would be fun and informative, but my father has to catch a plane for San Francisco tomorrow morning early."

I catch his eye, put an ounce of heat behind my words. "Maybe you could talk to him about me. He expressed an interest in my knowledge of Suzama's connection to Isis."

James blinks a few times. He must have a strong will; he does not immediately jump at my suggestion.

"I could talk to him. But as you can see he is not as young as he once was. I worry about tiring him unnecessarily."

I do not want to push James too hard. There is always the possibility I might damage him in some way. Since my rebirth as a vampire, I have found the power in my eyes particularly biting. I use it in small doses. But I do not want Dr. Seter to just walk away. I decide to let a portion of my ancient knowledge drop, but in the form of a lie. Making a drama of it, I pull James Seter aside and speak in hushed tones.

"Your Suzama scripture is not the only one in

existence," I say. "I have another one, but I think it is different. I would be happy to trade information with your father."

James pauses a moment to take this all in. "You can't be serious?"

I speak evenly. "But I am. If your father will meet with me, I would be happy to talk to him about it." I pause. "He will know within a minute whether I have discovered something authentic."

"He will want to question you before spending time with you."

I shake my head. "I will not talk here about what I have found. But please assure your father that I'm not a crackpot."

"Where do you want to meet?"

"There's a coffee shop three blocks from the ocean near Ocean Avenue and the freeway. I can meet you there in, say, half an hour."

That is the coffee shop where my beloved Ray came back to me, where he in fact returned to life. He appeared just after I shot two men to death after they'd tried to rape me. I was covered with a fine spray of blood at the time, a fitting ornament for dark delusions. I have not been back to the coffee shop since, but for some perverse reason I want to go there tonight. Maybe another phantom will appear to spice up my life. Yet I hope not. The pain of the last one is still an open wound for me. Just the thought of Ray fills me with sorrow. James is studying me.

"When you came here tonight," he says, "you acted like you had no knowledge of Suzama. Why?"

I reach out and straighten his tie. "If you knew what I know, James, you would make a point of appearing ignorant." I pause. "Tell your father to come. I will be waiting."

A half hour later I sit in the coffee shop across from Dr. Seter and his son. They have come alone, which is good. Actually it is good that they have come at all, but I suspect son dragged father along. The doctor doesn't look at me as if he expects to receive any divine revelation from me. But he does seem to be enjoying the apple pie and ice cream I've ordered for him. When you're a cute five-thousand-year-old blond, you can get away with murder.

"James tells me you're a student of archeology," Dr. Seter says as he forks up a heaping piece of pie. He has taken off the tie he wore to his lecture but otherwise he is dressed the same. His manner is relaxed, a scholar enjoying himself after giving a lecture he has obviously given a thousand times before. Briefly I wonder about his motivation for publicizing the Suzama scripture. I don't think he can be making much money from doing so. The cost of his book is nominal and he doesn't teach any high-priced seminar. He seems like a nice man with no hidden agenda.

"I am a student of Suzama," I say seriously. "I was not boasting when I said I possess a manuscript of hers."

Dr. Seter is amused. "Where did you find this manuscript?"

"Where did you find yours?" I ask.

"I have explained why I am reluctant to reveal that information."

"I have the same reluctance for the same reasons," I say.

He returns to his pie. He thinks I am a nice girl with nothing to say.

"Then I guess we'll just have to enjoy the food," he says politely.

I open his book to a photograph of a portion of the Suzama scripture. I point to the hieratic writing on the ancient papyrus.

"There are probably only two dozen people on Earth who can read this at a glance," I say. "You are one of them, I am another. This line says, 'The secret of the Goddess is in the sixteenth digit of the moon. Not the moon in the sky, but the moon in the high center. It is here the ambrosia of bliss is milked by the sincere seeker. It is only there the knowledge of the soul is revealed.'" I pause. "Is my translation accurate?"

Dr. Seter almost drops his fork. "How did you know that? I don't translate that line in the text."

"I told you, I am a student of Suzama."

James interrupts. "How do we know someone else didn't translate the line for you?"

"Because I can give you information that must be in the portion of your scripture that you keep hidden, as it is in mine. For example, I know of the four-word mantra Suzama used to invoke the white light from above the head, where the moon digit is really located. I know how the first word relates to the heart, the second to the throat, the third to the head. I know how the breath is synchronized with the mantra and that on the fourth word the divine white light of Isis is brought down into the human body."

Dr. Seter stares at me, stunned. "What is the four-word mantra?"

I speak seriously. "You know from your scripture that it is only to be revealed in private, at the time of initiation. I will not say it here. But you must realize by now that I know a great deal about Suzama's secret meditation practices. Therefore, it should be easy for you to believe that I must have access to another scripture belonging to her." I pause. "Am I correct?"

Dr. Seter studies me. "You know something, that's for sure. Frankly, I would be very curious to see your scripture."

"You have to show me yours first," I say. "I will be able to tell if it is authentic."

"How?" James interrupts.

I smile for him. "I will compare it to mine."

"Do you believe your scripture is identical to mine?" Dr. Seter asks.

"No. Yours speaks of a danger to the new master. Mine does not address that point." I add, "You lied when you said your scripture did not specify what the danger is."

Dr. Seter sits back. "How do you know that?"

"It doesn't matter. It's true." I pause. "Tell me how the danger is described?"

"I'm afraid that's not possible," James says. "Only inner members of our group are given such information."

"Ah," I say. "This inner group you have organized, what's its purpose? To protect the child once it is found?" By their reaction I see I have scored a bulls-eye. "Isn't that rather presumptuous of you? To think the messiah needs your protection?"

Dr. Seter is having trouble keeping up with me. Still, I have his full attention. "What if the scripture itself says he will need protection?" he asks.

"Does it?" I ask.

Dr. Seter hesitates. "Yes."

He is telling the truth, or at least the truth he knows.

"Father," James interrupts. "Should we be talking about these things in front of a stranger whom we have just met?"

Dr. Seter shrugs. "Isn't it obvious she knows as much about Suzama as we do?"

"But I don't," I say again. "I know different things about her. I am working with different source material. But back to your group, and how they will be used to protect the child. How exactly is that going to work?"

"Surely you can understand that we can't divulge the inner workings of our group," Dr. Seter says. "Not the way the government is scrutinizing every spiritual group in the country, searching for the next crazy cult. Please, let's try to keep this on an academic level. I would like to see your material, you would like to see mine. Fine, how can we work a place and a date to exchange information?"

"I told you," I say. "You have to show me yours first. If I am convinced it is authentic, I will show you what I have."

Dr. Seter is suspicious. "Why not have a simultaneous exchange?"

I smile warmly. "I will not harm your material. I'm sure when you show it to me there will be a dozen of your well-dressed boys and girls gathered around." I pause. "I suspect you travel with it. Why don't you show it to me tonight? I will not have to study it long to reach a conclusion."

Dr. Seter and James exchange a long look. "What could it hurt?" the doctor says finally, testing the waters.

James is unsure. He continues to study me. "How do we know you don't work for the FBI?"

I throw my head back and laugh. "Where will you find a FBI agent who can read hieroglyphics?"

"But you are curious about the purpose of our group?" James persists. "These are the kinds of questions the government might ask."

I catch James's eye and let my power out in a measured dose. "I am not from the government. I represent no one other than myself. My interest in the Suzama material is motivated only by the highest and best desires." I pause and catch the eye of the doctor as well. "Let me see it. You will have no regrets."

Dr. Seter touches his son's arm as he nods in answer to my request. "We don't exactly travel with it, but it's not far from here." He pauses. "It's out in Palm Springs."

"Palm Springs," I mutter. What a coincidence. One passes through Palm Springs on the way to Joshua Tree National Monument, where Paula supposedly conceived her child. I have been meaning to go out there for some time.

"James can show you the scripture tomorrow morning," Dr. Seter says, checking his watch. "It's too late to see it tonight."

I stand. "But I'm a night girl. And I would like you to be there, Dr. Seter, when I examine it. If you please? Let's go now."

He is taken aback by my boldness and gazes up at me. "May I ask how old you are, Alisa?"

I smile. "You must know that Suzama was not very old when she wrote your scripture."

Dr. Seter shakes his head. "I didn't know that. How old was she?"

"I take that back. I'm not sure how old she was when she wrote it. I only know she died before her twentieth birthday."

I don't add, like me.

Some, of course, consider vampires the walking dead.

3

Before heading for Palm Springs, I leave Seymour a message on the answering machine in our new home in Pacific Palisades. We stay in regular contact. It's a promise we keep to each other. I have left him before in the middle of the night without explanation and have promised never to do it again. Also, my daughter, Kalika, still walks the streets, and it is impossible to tell when she will come for us again. Seymour and I, we cover each other's backs. But I feel in my heart it will not be long before I see Kalika again. A part of me senses that she has yet to find the child, but is searching constantly for him. I have to wonder if my intuition about her is attached to the psychic thread that connects all mothers to their children.

Dr. Seter and James drive ahead of me on the long road to Palm Springs. They have an old white Volvo, I a brand-new red Porsche. James is behind the wheel. I keep only fifty feet behind, just off to their right in the fast lane. They would be surprised to know that I can hear them as they speak. Yet it is only when we have been on the road an hour that they finally begin to talk. Before then Dr. Seter had been slipping in and out of sleep.

James: "Why are we doing this?"

Dr. Seter: "Do you think we should just ignore her?"

James: "Not at all. I'm as curious about her as you. Remember it was I who insisted upon the meeting. But I think we should investigate her background before letting her see the scripture."

Dr. Seter: "What harm can she do to it? She will not be able to translate a fraction of the hieroglyphics without hours of time. I don't care how well versed she is in the field." A pause. "She must be older than she looks. It takes years to learn to read the way she did."

James: "I'm sure she's older than she looks. Notice she didn't actually tell you her age?"

Dr. Seter: "What are you saying? That she has mastered Suzama's practices and managed to reverse her age?"

James: "It's possible. She knew enough about the high initiation."

Dr. Seter: "That's what startled me about her, too. There are few people in our group who know about that." A pause. "She must be telling the truth. She must have another text."

James: "I agree. But she's evasive. I don't trust her. I want full security when we show her the papyrus."

Dr. Seter: "Of course. You've called ahead? They know we're coming?"

James: "Yes. The whole group will be there."

Dr. Seter: "Really? Why? We don't need all of them there. The others should be on their way to San Francisco."

James: "I told you, I don't trust this girl." A pause. "But I have another reason."

Dr. Seter: "What?"

James: "I wonder if Alisa has direct knowledge about the child."

Dr. Seter: "Now you're speculating."

James: "I'm not so sure. She seemed particularly concerned about the child being harmed." A pause. "Maybe I say that backward. I wonder if she already knows about the Dark Mother."

I almost drive off the road. They are talking about Kalika.

My daughter? Did Suzama brand her as evil five thousand years ago?

Dr. Seter: "I didn't get that impression."

James: "Can I say something really off the wall?"

Dr. Seter: "It's a long drive. We may as well discuss every possibility."

James: "What if this Alisa is working for the Black Mother?"

Dr. Seter laughs: "She hardly seems the type, do you think?"

James: "Consider. She looks like a twenty-year-old, but she appears to have the education of someone who has studied for thirty years. Also, her manner is curious. Notice the way she catches your eye, and then says things you have trouble resisting."

Dr. Seter laughs some more: "I never noticed that. I think you are the one who is having trouble resisting her."

James: "I don't know. I just hope we're not leading her to the child by letting her study the scripture."

Dr. Seter: "But there's nothing in the scripture that points to where the child is at this time, except perhaps still in California."

James: "To us maybe. But she may find clues in the text we have missed." A pause. "I pray to God we're not doing anything to endanger the child further. From the descriptions I have read of the Dark Mother, I wouldn't want anyone, friend or foe, to run into her. I think that kind of evil lives to kill."

Dr. Seter: "But you know, son, we have spent the last ten years preparing to meet her." A pause. "It's inevitable, if we're to believe half of what we've read."

James: "Do you really think we're the ones chosen to defend the child?"

Dr. Seter: "I wouldn't have bought so many automatic weapons unless I did." A sigh. "I'm more worried that Alisa may be from the government than that she represents the Dark Mother."

James: "Then why show her anything?"

Dr. Seter: "As I said, it can cause no harm. She will not have time to translate the portions of the scripture we don't want her to translate. And she will find nothing in our center the government would be excited about."

James: "I hope you're right." A pause. "She is incredibly beautiful."

Dr. Seter: "I noticed."

I find their private conversation fascinating.

The center they have referred to is a large house in an area clearly zoned for both business and residential properties. There are many cars parked along the street as we pull up. Like Dr. Seter, I am surprised that James has directed the whole group here, especially when they have a lecture the following night in San Francisco. Yet James's intuitions about me are shockingly accurate. He wonders if the Dark Mother has sent me. How would he feel if he knew I am the Dark Mother's mother? I would have a hard time convincing him I'm on his side, not hers.

Yet the one thing I have learned by eavesdropping is that the Suzama Society is there to protect the child, not harm it. Still, the reference to automatic weapons disturbs me. It is true that they might come in handy should Kalika show up, but I know guns in the hands of true believers seldom get pointed in the right direction at the right time.

What is the source of James's excellent intuition? Perhaps it is a result of following Suzama's meditation practices. I found his reference to reversed aging intriguing. Is James older than he looks? I remember Suzama's often saying that aging is a product of lower consciousness, and immortality the gift of highest consciousness.

Dr. Seter and James welcome me warmly as I climb from my car.

"Did you have a pleasant drive?" Seter asks.

"I listened to loud music the whole way," I say, gesturing to all the cars. "Is there another lecture here tonight?"

Dr. Seter glances at James. "Many in our group have returned here to collect supplies for the remainder of my tour," the doctor explains. "I have to fly to the East Coast after my San Francisco lecture." He gestures to the house. "Please come in. Would you like some coffee?"

"Thank you, no. I am wide awake."

"That's right," James says, moving up behind us. "You're a night person."

Inside there are two dozen navy blue suits, half and half, pants and skirts, male and female, all young and attractive. I don't get the uniform thing, especially around Dr. Seter, who seems so laid back. Perhaps it is James's idea, although he seems far from a fanatic. The group studies me as I step into the huge house. The place is orderly, the furniture traditional, every corner clean and dust free. There is a faint odor of fried chicken in the air, mashed potatoes, and broccoli. They are not vegetarians, even though Suzama was.

Staring at the innocent faces, I wonder if they practice using their automatic weapons deep in the desert when no one is around. Simply to own an automatic weapon is to invite a felony charge, jail time. Dr. Seter must be convinced the enemy is at hand to go to such extremes. Of course, who am I to judge? He has not fed the enemy another person's blood in the middle of the night just to get her to stop crying. My dear daughter—my how fast she grew and how strong. She can kick my ass in a fight. That, I know from experience.

The memory of Eric Hawkins, Kalika's personal snack bar, is never far.

"Oh God, I'm bleeding! She's cut my neck! The blood is gushing out! Help me!"

But I could not help him. I was only able to use him.

A young woman about my apparent age steps forward to shake my hand. "My name is Lisa," she says. "You're Alisa?"

"Yes."

"We hear you can read hieroglyphics?"

"Hieroglyphics and comic books have always been favorites of mine," I say. There is a murmur of laughter. "Where are you from, Lisa?"

"North Dakota. I met Dr. Seter there last year—"

"Lisa is our accountant," Dr. Seter interrupts. "I call her boss."

The group laughs. They obviously love the man.

I am led down into a basement. Few homes in Southern California have basements, and this one is special, to say the least. As James closes the door behind us, I notice that it has a rubber seal all around it. Almost immediately I notice a change in the air pressure, and I understand why. They are worried about dust and dampness and the effect they would have on the scripture. The air in the basement is carefully filtered.

Six of the group have followed me into the basement, including James and Dr. Seter. A young man named Charles steps to a vault at the far end of the basement. In the center of the room is a large white table with brilliant overhead lights and a double ocular over-size microscope at one end. There are also a couple of magnifying glasses and loupes sitting handily by. Charles spins the steel knob on the vault, dialing the combination. His body is between me and the knob but I listen closely and in a moment I know the combination, R48, L32, R16, L17, R12, L10.

The vault pops open. Charles lifts out a pale yellow sheet of papyrus wrapped in acid-free tissue paper and carries it to the table to set down under the bright lights. The scripture is a foot across, two feet long. A rush of excitement makes my heart pound. Even through the covering tissue paper, I smell ancient Egypt!

I recognize the hieratic writing.

It is tiny, carefully crafted.

It is definitely in Suzama's cursive.

Dr. Seter gestures for me to examine it closer after he lifts off the tissue paper.

As I bend over the table, he has no idea I am about to read it much faster than he would read a large-print book. Yet James stands close beside me, his eyes on mine.

I begin to read.

I am Suzama and my words are true. The past and the future are the same to my illumined vision. You who read these words are warned not to doubt what is recorded lest you fall into error and lose your way on the path. I am Suzama and I speak for the truth.

The lord of creation is both inside and outside creation. He is like the sap in the flower, the space in an empty room. He is always present but unseen. His joy shines like the sun in the sky, his will swims like a fish beneath the ocean. He cannot be known by the mind or even the heart. Only the inner silence recognizes him.

He is both male and female and he is neither. To speak of him as one or the other is only a manner of speaking. In order to protect the righteous and destroy the wicked, he takes birth again and again throughout the ages.

His most recent birth was as Sri Krishna in the land of the Pandu brothers. Then and there he slew demons and granted realization to the worthy. His life lasted 135 years, from 3675 to 3810. He will be remembered as the divine personality.

His next birth will be as Adi Shankara in the land of the Vedas. Then and there he will make available the knowledge of the Brahman, the highest reality. His life will last 32 years, from 6111 to 6143. He will be well remembered as the divine teacher.

His subsequent birth will be as Jesus of Nazareth in the land of Abraham. Then and there he will embody and teach perfect love and compassion. His life will last 108 years, from

7608 to 7716. He will be well remembered as the divine savior.

The scripture ends there. I look over at Dr. Seter. "Where's the rest of it?" I ask.

"You do not need all of it to judge its authenticity," Dr. Seter says.

"That doesn't answer my question," I say.

"The rest of it is in the vault," James interrupts, close to my right side. "But we decided it wouldn't be a good idea to bring it all out tonight."

On the road, I was briefly separated from them by a distance of two hundred feet. At that point they had their radio on and their windows up. Even I, with my supernatural hearing, could not hear what they were saying. They must have made this decision at that time. Naturally, I am disappointed not to see it all. Yet I am thrilled by what I have read. Already I am convinced the scripture is authentic. The papyrus even feels as if it is five thousand years old. I stroke it gently, making James jump.

"Don't do that," he says.

I withdraw my hand. "I know how to handle such things. I did not harm it in any way." I pause and look at the doctor. "It is my belief that this scripture is authentic."

Dr. Seter is taken back. "You can tell that by such a brief study?"

"Yes. This portion matches what I have. I take back what I said earlier. They're almost identical." I pause. "It would help us if I could see the rest."

Dr. Seter is apologetic. "Alisa, surely you understand what an act of good faith it was for us to show you what we have shown you. Now it's only right, before we reveal any more, that you show us at least a portion of what you have discovered." He pauses and smiles. "I think that is fair. Don't you?"

"Very fair. May I have a day or two to deliver the material to you?"

"Certainly," Dr. Seter says. "James will not be accompanying me east. You can bring what you wish to show us here and he will have a look at it."

"Fine," I say. "But you must look at it yourself, Dr. Seter."

"But I have told you about my commitments on the East Coast."

"What I have to show you will make those commitments seem unimportant."

Dr. Seter is troubled. "I am not willing to cancel any of my lectures until I have more proof."

"I will give you such proof before you leave for the East. Where will you be staying in San Francisco?"

"At the Hilton by the airport," James says. "You can leave a message there. We'll return your call promptly."

I offer Dr. Seter my hand. "I look forward to meeting you again soon."

The doctor is surprised at my sudden departure. "But you've said hardly anything about what we've shown you."

I keep my tone light. "It's what you haven't shown me that I would have a lot to say about."

James touches my arm. "I'll walk you out, Alisa, if you'd like."

I smile. "I would like that very much."

Outside James is a study in politeness.

"I hope you can understand our caution," he says. "We just met you tonight. While we're all impressed with your understanding of the Suzama material, we still have to take things one step at a time."

"No problem," I say as I open my car door. "I doubt that I would have been nearly as open as you and your father have been."

James smiles. "Actually, Alisa, you haven't been very open." He pauses. "You can at least tell us where you found your material."

"In India."

He frowns. "Are you serious? Where?"

"In Sri Nagar."

He nods. "I know where that is. In the Himalayas. What were you doing there?"

"I had a few dreams of my own." I pause. "How old are you, James?"

"Twenty-eight."

"You look much younger. I am twenty-five, for your information."

"You look much younger," he says. "Do you practice anything Suzama taught?"

I smile. "A personal question. I don't know if I want to answer that."

"Come on," he insists.

"I'll tell you what, I'll make a deal with you. Tell me what you practice and I'll tell you what I practice."

He gives a sheepish grin. "You're a clever young woman, Alisa. I don't know if it's smart to share too many secrets with you."

Before I climb into my car I place my palm on his chest. I catch his dark eyes once more, and for the first time I notice how deep they are, how beautiful. There is more to him than meets even my penetrating eyes. A soothing warmth sweeps over me, for him, as well as for his father. Beneath my soft hand his warm heart beats faster. He may not trust me, but I know he likes me, maybe even wants me.

It is strange how I suddenly want him. Since Ray, I have not really desired any man. Even with Joel and Arturo, it was more my love for them that bound me to them. Yet, out of the blue, James has me all hot and bothered. Seymour would be incredibly jealous.

"Secrets are what make us all interesting," I say, and give him a light peck on the cheek. "Have fun in San Francisco. I will call you."

He grabs my arm.

"There is something unusual about you, Alisa," he says in a gentle voice. "I'm going to figure out what it is."

I laugh. "And tell the whole world?"

He smiles, but when he speaks there is a seriousness in his voice. "I have a feeling few in the world would believe me."

4

The time is well after one, but I do not drive straight home. Being a vampire, I find one in the morning not unpleasant. Also, since my rebirth as a vampire, I have found I need little rest, an hour's nap here and there. Even when the sun is high in the daylight sky, my powers are hardly affected. Once again I attribute this to the fact that I used primarily Yaksha's blood to bring about my transformation.

And a few drops of Paula's child's blood.

I, like Seymour, have the influence of it in my life.

I drive to Joshua Tree National Monument, and when I arrive the moon is high in the sky. The park is large, and I have no idea where Paula sat when the brilliant blue light came out of the sky and blessed her. Only that she sat on a bluff watching the sunset. After the blue light left and the sun rose the next morning, the surrounding Joshua trees were larger.

"The Joshua trees around me—they were all taller."

"Are you sure?"

"Pretty sure. Some were twice the size they had been the evening before."

I park in a spot that catches my eye and get out and walk across the desert. The moonlight, as it pours over me, seems to seep into the crown of my head, and I am reminded of the time in the desert outside Las Vegas when I escaped a nuclear explosion by filling my body with moonlight and floating high into the sky. As I prowl the sandy terrain among the Joshua trees that stand like sentinels from another age, I feel my step lighten. It is almost as if I can bob off the ground, and that possibility fills me with excitement. To fly up with the stars and escape the prison of my problems. My bare arms begin to glow with a milky white radiance. I can almost see through them.

Then I see the place. My recognition of it is immediate. I do not even have to take note of the tall surrounding trees to confirm my belief. I simply know it is the spot. A feeling of tranquillity, of sanctity even, radiates from the place. It draws me forward. Clearly something momentous occurred here. In a minute I am standing atop the bluff where I am convinced Paula conceived her child. I lift my arms to the stars.

"Suzama!" I call. "Show me what you saw!"

There is no answer, at least no obvious one. Yet I am suddenly overcome by a wave of fatigue, and I sit down to close my eyes and meditate with the rhythm of the breath and the secret mantra. Soon white light is pouring, not from above, but from a place inside me, and I am lost in memories of nights of wonder and terror at the feet of a tender clairvoyant, who saw not only the birth of God, but the death as well. There was, of course, a reason Suzama died so young, and perhaps I was a part of that reason.

When I arrived in Egypt, it was fifty years after the death of Lord Krishna, fifty years into the dark age, what was to become known as Kali Yuga. Following the trail of adventurous merchants, who traveled the Far East thousands of years before Marco Polo was born, I arrived in an Egypt that to my eyes was infinite in splendor and riches. Truthfully, it overwhelmed me, although I was also relieved to be out of India, where Yaksha was in the midst of a bloody rampage to destroy every living vampire, as part of a vow he had made to Krishna.

The bright sun was hard on a young vampire like me. Riding into the enchanted city on the back of a camel, I had to keep my head covered with many layers of cloth. The sun burned into my brain, sapping every ounce of my strength. Yet the sight of the Great Pyramid, four times larger than the present-day pyramid that bears the same name, filled me with wonder. Covered with shiny white ivory and capped with glistening gold, it stole my breath away. All I could think as the bright rays heated my already boiling blood was to escape into its dark interior, rest, and try to forget the many trials of my journey. I thought it more than a coincidence that one of the first people I met when I entered the magical city was Suzama herself.

She was far from a high priestess that day. Only sixteen, with long dark hair and eyes as bright as they were kind, she wore a slave's simple garment. I saw her bending over the bank of the Nile to collect water in a large clay jar. On my exhausted camel, moving slowly toward her, I thought she seemed to stiffen. She glanced over her shoulder at me, almost as if she felt me approach. Later she was to tell me that she'd already had many visions of my coming. As our eyes met, my heart beat faster. I could remember no dream I'd had about her, but I knew her face was one I would never forget awake or asleep.

Suzama was not merely beautiful, although she would have been considered attractive in any age or place. Her allure came from the marks that austerity and pain had stamped on her young beauty, marks that made her enchanting, not repulsive. It was as if she had witnessed a thousand lives of suffering and come to a realization that transcended mortal acceptance. She was both saintly and sensual. Her lips so generous, she had only to smile to make you feel kissed. I loved her when I saw her, and until then I had never loved anyone on sight, except for Krishna himself.

She offered me a drink from her jug.

"I am called Suzama," she said. "Who are you?"

"Sita," I answered, giving her my real name. I drank the water hungrily, and splashed some on my dusty face. The Nile was cool and sweet in those days. I don't know what has become of it now. "I am new here."

But Suzama shook her head. "You have always been here." Then she touched her heart and I saw tears in her eyes. "I know you, Sita. You have great power."

This was my first sign of her power. Suzama knew things from inside herself, not from outside. Indeed, later, I came to believe the entire world was a dream to her. Yet paradoxically it could still cause her intense pain. Her deepest feelings were enigmatic, dispassionately unattached, but at the same time passionately involved. When she took my hand and led me in the direction of her family, I felt I had been touched by an angel. Yet I did not know that for the next three and a half years, I would hardly ever leave her sight. Her mystical mission had not yet begun, but soon it would hit like a bolt of lightning. And I would be her thunder.

5

The next morning I have been only seconds in my expensive and exquisitely furnished tri-level home in Pacific Palisades when the phone rings. Upstairs I hear Seymour snoring peacefully, yet the call makes me anxious. Our number is unlisted. Who would know to call? And so early in the morning?

I pick up the phone and hold it close.

"Hello?"

There is a pause. Then the soft voice, the gentle inflections.

"It is I," she says.

The blood freezes in my veins. "Kalika."

"Yes, Mother, you remember me. That is good. How have you been?"

"Fine. How are you?"

"Wonderful. Busy."

"You haven't found him yet," I say. "You're not going to find him."

Kalika could be smiling. "You are wrong. I haven't found him but I am going to find him. You are going to help me."

"I hardly think so."

"You think too much. Your thoughts blind you. I told you I'm not going to harm the child. I'm your daughter. You should believe me. I believe you even when I hear you lying to me."

"Where are you?" I ask.

"Not far. I'm high up. I have a view. You would enjoy it."

"How did you get this number?"

"It wasn't difficult." A pause. "I saw you last night at that boring meeting. I saw you talking to those people."

If possible, my blood grows colder. Just by meeting and talking to people, I put them suddenly in danger. It does not seem fair that I should love someone who causes me such grief. Yes, I am chilled by Kalika's call, and grateful for it as well. How hopeless mothers are.

"Those people are no concern of yours," I say harshly.

"I think the doctor is a nice man. But I see you like the son. Handsome devil, isn't he?" A pause. "Is it appropriate for a daughter to comment on the company her mother keeps?"

"No."

She laughs softly. "Nothing is as it seems. Black

can appear white when the light is blinding. But white loses all luster at the faintest sign of darkness. Why trust them when you can trust me?"

"Because you are a coldblooded murderer."

"Oh. We all have our faults. When did you become so judgmental?"

My tone is bitter. "You know when."

"I suppose. How is Seymour?"

"He's dead."

"That was his corpse at the lecture last night?"

I sigh. "He's fine, no thanks to you."

"See. I can be merciful. I am a mother as well, you know."

"You called Paula. You faked my voice, and even so she did not call you back."

"That is true," Kalika says. "But Suzama would know how to set up a meeting with Paula. She might have spelled that out in her book. You knew her, didn't you?"

I hesitate. "Yes."

"And you still think fondly of her. But to this day you do not know what destroyed her."

"She was destroyed in the big earthquake, along with the Setians. Her death is no mystery to me."

"But who were those Setians? You stared them straight in the eye and did not recognize them."

"I knew they were evil, in the end."

She mocks me. "But too late to save Suzama."

"Why do you talk about them? Or are you just up to your old tricks? The master manipulator trying to confuse the issue. If you want to come for me, fine. Come now, I tire of your games. You don't scare me."

Kalika is a long time answering. While I wait for her next words, I listen closely and hear in the background, not far from where Kalika is, the splash of water. My daughter must be near an open window, standing on a balcony perhaps. There is definitely a swimming pool in her vicinity. It is far below her I believe. There are many people in it, children playing with a ball, laughing and shouting, and more serious athletes swimming serious laps. I hear the latter turn in the water as they finish each lap and push off the walls. I count the strokes, and there are many of them. It is a large pool. There are not many such large pools in the Los Angeles area. I should be able to get a list of them.

Kalika finally speaks.

"I do not want to harm you, Mother. I am here for the child. But if you stand in my way, I cannot promise you that you or your darling Seymour will survive." She adds, "That is not a threat, merely an observation."

"Thank you. I feel much better. Why did you call?"

"To hear your voice. For some reason your voice carries special meaning to me."

"I don't believe that," I say.

"It is true."

"And the other reason for your call?"

"If I tell you that it will spoil all the fun." A pause. "Is there anything I can do for you, Mother?"

"Leave Dr. Seter and his people alone. Leave the child alone."

Kalika hesitates. "I'm afraid I can't do that. Is there anything else you want?"

I slump against the wall, exhausted. "You know, Kalika, the night you were born was hard for me. The delivery was agonizing and I lost a lot of blood. I almost died, and even when I held you in my arms and looked into your eyes I was scared. Even then I knew you were not normal, not even by vampire standards. But despite all that a part of me was happy, happier than I had ever been in my life. I didn't realize this until later. I had wanted a daughter and now I had one. God gave you to me, I thought, and I thanked him for you." I have to take a breath. "Do you understand what I am saying?"

"Yes."

"You are what you are. Your nature is to kill, and I understand that because I'm a killer as well. But over the centuries I have learned to control that instinct. Now I only kill when it is necessary. You can learn to do the same." I pause. "That is what I ask of you. Only that."

She considers. When she speaks next, her voice is particularly soft. It is almost as if she is speaking inside my brain. And I find her words strangely moving.

"I can do that for you, Mother. But my list of who can live and who must die is vastly different from yours. The phantom, Ray, was one of your illusions, one of your *mayas*. Your desire to have your child Lalita reborn is still a maya for you. You refuse to let it go. That is why you were given me as your daughter—one of the reasons. But anyone who sees through the veil of maya cannot fathom the divine will. The veil is stained and the absolute is without flaw. One cannot reveal the other. In the same way, I am your own daughter but you cannot fathom me."

I have to shake myself to resist her subtle spell. My memory reminds me that she is using me.

"Was torturing Eric to death part of God's will?" I ask.

She speaks matter-of-factly. "I did what I did to Eric to inspire you to tell me the location of the child." A pause. "Besides, he was not well. He was going to die anyway. His next birth will be more auspicious."

I snort. "Of course he was not well! You had been drinking his blood night and day! He died in horrible pain, in your hands!"

"So he did, and he stained my dress." She laughs again. "Goodbye, Mother. Don't think about what I have told you. It will only confuse you more. Just have faith in your darling daughter. It is the only thing now that can save you from suffering much greater pain."

Kalika hangs up the phone.

6

As Seymour comes down for his breakfast, I am sitting at the kitchen table. I have made him bacon and eggs and toast, his favorite high-cholesterol meal. He has on a brown robe and is fresh from a warm shower. He smiles at me as I pour his hand-squeezed orange juice from the other side of the table.

"One day you're going to make somebody a great wife," he says.

"Thank you. One day you're going to make a girl have a nervous breakdown."

"You worry about me too much. I just went to the movies. God knows where you were." He picks up his fork and tests his eggs. "Did you get me the morning paper? You know I can't enjoy my food unless I'm fully informed on current events," he jokes.

I speak seriously. "I am your morning paper."

He butters his toast. "What's the matter? Did Suzama predict that I am the next messiah?"

"The scripture is authentic."

"You saw it?"

"A piece of it. Suzama wrote it."

He puts down his butter knife. "But how come you never saw her working on it?"

"I was with her most of the time, but not every second. She could have written it on any number of days."

"But she didn't talk to you about it? And you were her best friend?"

"She never talked about it to me. But Suzama kept her own counsel. I doubt if she spoke to anyone about the scripture. But she left it in a place where it could be found—at a time she wished it to be found."

Seymour considers. "How did you talk Dr. Seter into letting you see it?"

There is an edge to his question.

"Are you asking if I slept with his son?"

"I noticed you were talking to him after you told me to get lost."

"I didn't tell you to get lost. I told you to go have fun." I pause. "I convinced both son and father that I have a similar scripture. They want to see it soon."

"Great. We can make one up this afternoon. We

can make papyrus and age it in the sun, then you can give me a lesson in drawing hieroglyphics." He pauses. "It wasn't a very inventive lie."

"It served its purpose." I frown. "I will have to give them something substantial to make them let me see the remainder of the scripture."

"Why don't you just give them me to use as a human sacrifice?"

"Stop that. They are not such a bad bunch." Then I have to smile. "But they are busy practicing with automatic weapons in the desert."

"They sound like a nice all-American cult."

"No, I don't think they're that, but they really do have guns. I heard the Seters talk about them when they didn't think I was listening." I pause. "But those guns might come in handy."

"Why?"

"Kalika called."

This shocks him. "When?"

"A half hour ago."

"Did she call here?"

"Yes."

He has lost his appetite for his breakfast and sits, staring out the window, his face pale. In the distance is the blue Pacific. Only he and I know how red the water can run when it is diluted with blood. Yet I remind myself that Seymour doesn't remember exactly what Kalika did to him. The time has come, I know, to tell him. Many things.

"How did she get our number?" he mutters.

"Who knows? She gets what she wants."

"If she has our number she has our address. She could be on her way here now."

I shake my head. "If she just wanted to kill us, I don't think she would have called first."

"Why did she call then?"

"She said she wanted to hear my voice."

"Like Hitler used to call home to talk to mom?" he asks.

"She hasn't found the child. She wants me to help her find him."

"But you don't know where the kid is."

"She knows that. Still, she seems to feel I can lead her to the Paula and the baby."

Seymour is puzzled. I can see the question coming.

"You must have some idea what is so special about this child?"

I pour myself a glass of orange juice. I have drunk blood only three times since my rebirth as a vampire, and none of my snacks were any the worse for wear in the morning. I suspect, toward the end of his life, that Yaksha did not need blood at all to survive. Still, it tasted good to me, the warm red elixir, better than the orange juice I now sip.

"This child could be the one spoken of in the Suzama scriptures," I say softly.

Seymour stares at me. "You've got to be kidding?"

"No."

He is annoyed. "That's ridiculous. All right, I believe in vampires. I believe in you. I even believe in your bad-tempered daughter. But I don't believe that Jesus was just born in a hospital in Los Angeles. I'm sorry but I can't. It's too weird."

"Do you remember what happened to you after Kalika threw you off the pier?"

He hesitates. "Yeah. The water was freezing and I got hypothermia and passed out and you came to my rescue."

"Where did you regain consciousness?"

"Up in the mountains. The next morning."

"You were unconscious for a long time, don't you think?"

"So? What does this have to do with this kid?"

I speak carefully. "Seymour, you did not simply pass out in the cold water. Kalika did not let you go so easily. She threw something at you, a sharp stake. It was shaped like a spear." I pause. "She threw it so hard it stabbed through your spine and out through your stomach."

Seymour stands. "That's not true."

"It is true. I jumped off the pier and helped you to shore, as I told you. But you were on the beach less than a minute when you finally lost consciousness."

He is agitated. "Then how did the wound disappear? You told me you didn't give me any of your vampire blood."

"At the time I intended to give you my blood. But I was afraid to pull out the stake. I thought it would kill you." I shrug. "So I left it in."

He is breathing hard. "You're not answering my questions."

I stand and step to his side and put a hand on his shoulder.

"You lost too much blood. Even I couldn't save you." I pause. "You died that night on that beach."

He forces a smile. "Yeah, right. I'm Lazarus, back from the dead."

"There was a vial of the child's blood. I stole it from the nurse who was caring for the baby at the hospital. I had that vial with me when I took you up to the mountains."

"Why did you take me up there? You never explained that."

"To cremate your body. You must remember that when you woke up you were lying on a huge pile of wood." I squeeze his shoulder. "Seymour."

He jumps back and trembles. "That's not possible. You're making this story up. I couldn't have been dead. When you're dead you're dead. God damn it, Sita, don't lie to me this way. You're scaring me and I don't like it."

I am patient. "Just before I lit the wood, a strange feeling swept over me. I was looking down at you and I was holding this burning lighter and I couldn't stop staring at your face and thinking how you shouldn't be dead. Then I remembered the vial of blood, and I took it out of my pocket and poured some over your wounds and some down your throat. Then I walked away and stood behind a tree and prayed to God that everything would be all right." I move to his side again and put my arm over his shoulder. Both our eyes are damp. "And you were all right, Seymour. It was a miracle. You were sitting there and everything was perfectly all right." I kiss the side of his face and whisper in his ear. "I wouldn't lie to you about this, you know. I don't lie to those I love."

He is still shaking. "But I don't remember any of this."

"Maybe that is part of the miracle. Maybe it is for the best."

He looks at me with a sad little boy's face. "She really killed me?"

"Yes."

"And that baby's blood brought me back?"

"Yes."

He is awed as well as shocked. "That must mean . . ." He can't finish.

"Yes." I bury my face against his chest and dry my eyes on his robe. "I can't let my daughter get to him or to Paula. I just can't. I have to stop her and the only way I can do that is to kill her."

Seymour strokes my hair. Now he comforts me. We make a fine pair.

"Can she be killed?" he asks.

I raise my head. "I think so. Even Yaksha could be killed."

"But she is more powerful than Yaksha. You said so yourself."

I turn away and look at the ocean out the window.

"She must drink blood to survive," I say. "She has needs that only mortal flesh can fulfill. A portion of her must be mortal. She must be vulnerable."

"To the fire of automatic weapons?" He is recovering from the shock. His inner strength never ceases to amaze me. But he is a believer now, even if he won't admit it. Perhaps Lazarus argued that he had never been dead. For God's sake, Jesus, it was just a bad cold. Yeah, well, why do you smell so bad, Laz?

I continue to stand with my back to Seymour.

"I have thought of enlisting their aid," I say. "But to do so I would have to tell them an awful lot, maybe even what I am. I might have to give them a demonstration."

"You don't want to do that. They'd kill you after they killed Kalika, just to be on the safe side." Seymour considers. "Kalika is described in their scripture?"

"That's a perceptive question. Yes. But they haven't let me read that portion of the scripture. I only know of their knowledge of Kalika because I eavesdropped on their conversation."

"Did they call her Kalika?"

"The Dark Mother. It is the same difference." I grimace. "They have a horrible opinion of her."

"No doubt. Especially if Suzama was as accurate as you say." Seymour scratches his head. "You can't tell them that you're a vampire and knew Suzama personally. You would have to drink some blood in front of them to get them to listen to you after that, and then they would go running for their guns. But if you're able to describe Kalika in clear enough terms, they might believe you enough to check her out. How many of them are there?"

"Two dozen, which is a small army if they have the guns I think they do."

"You can give them some of your high-tech weapons."

"I've thought of that as well," I say.

"The only problem is that you don't know where your daughter is."

"That may not be true." I explain how Kalika spoke of her wonderful view, and the large pool below her. Yet this tip only seems to disturb Seymour.

"She mentioned the view," he says. "She went to the trouble to stand out on a balcony when she spoke to you. She knows all about your phenomenal hearing. And she probably knows how few places fit the description of her current residence. Does this add up to something in your mind?"

"A trap, of course. She might be lying in wait for us."

"She might be lying in wait for the entire Suzama Society. If she was watching you last night, she might suspect you will turn to them for help."

"I don't know if she takes them seriously. She called last night's lecture boring." I pause. "Plus she promised she wouldn't kill unless it was necessary."

"Oh, that's a relief. I feel a whole lot better now. The Mother of Darkness promises her vampire mother she's not going to get rough unless she gets pushed around. If I understand you correctly, the Suzama Society thinks it is their destiny to kill Kalika. Well, your daughter's not going to stand around and let them fill her full of lead."

I shake my head. "Kalika is many things, but I don't think she would have said such a thing to me unless it was true."

"By that reasoning you should believe she has no intention of harming the child."

"No. Obviously she intends to kill the child. She has killed to try to get to him. She is not some star-struck devotee who wants to gaze upon him in wonder. But her promise to me was something else. In fact, she asked if there was anything she could do for me."

"Still, the Suzama gang will have to hit her hard and quick if they're to survive."

"Agreed. But should we go to them for help? Should we risk their lives? Do we have the right?"

He shrugs. "It's their decision."

"Don't be so flip. No matter what you or I tell them, they won't understand how deadly Kalika is until they come face to face with her."

"I meant what I said. Their decision would not be flip. This is something these people believe in. They have dedicated their lives to it. Also, if all this is true, look at what's at stake? If this baby is the Big Guy then the world needs him. Kalika must be stopped, and I have to say no price is too high to stop her."

I nod sadly. "You said something similar when she was just a baby."

"Yes. And you wanted to give her a chance to see who she turned out to be." He pats me on the shoulder. "I'm sorry I have to put it that way. I just think we have to get a hold of all the firepower we can. Let's try to track down Kalika today. If we find her, and we live, then we'll go talk to Dr. Seter. He'll listen. It's just a question of how far you have to go to persuade him."

"Is there anything I can do for you, Mother?"

There is pain in my voice as I speak next.

"This child is special, there can be no question about that. But to me, Kalika, even if she is evil, is special as well." My head hangs heavy. "I don't know whether to pray for success or failure."

7

A local realtor informs me that there are only a dozen places in Los Angeles that fit my description of a tall apartment building with a large pool. The one with the largest pool is in Century City, at Century City Park East. Seymour and I decide to go there first. The place is exclusive, with twin towers that rise twenty stories into the sky. There is valet parking, a gym, and a tennis court beside the wonderful pool. I let the valet take the car, but I don't immediately head for the woman at the reception area.

"I appreciate what you said about this being a trap," I say to Seymour, who insisted on coming so that he could serve as lookout. "But the chances are she doesn't know we're here. I don't want to walk in and request her by name."

"Chances are she's working under a different name. Did you bring a picture of her?"

"Yes. I have several of her taken when she was fully grown. But I don't want to tip our hand. If we quiz the woman at the desk, and show her Kalika's picture, she may tell Kalika someone was looking for her. These people are trained to do that. I would rather check out the underground garage first. If Kalika has a car, it will probably be new and I should be able to smell her on it."

"She could be out," Seymour says.

"It is a possibility. But I want to do this first."

So we head underground. We're dressed properly, like rich sophisticates, so no one pays any attention to us. On the second garage level a new white Mercedes catches my eye. From where I am standing, forty feet away, I don't smell my daughter. Yet there is something about the car that draws my attention. I wonder if the vehicle is emitting *vibrations*. Certainly my daughter has a very powerful aura.

A moment later we have our hands on the car.

"If this is hers," Seymour says, "she has good taste."

"I need to smell the interior," I say.

Seymour points to a tiny flashing red light inside. "Don't set off the alarm."

"I see it," I mutter as I flex my palms over the driver's side window. Very slowly I begin to push the window down. A crack appears and I let go and stick my nose close to it. There is a faint musky odor, which, according to the Vedas, is Kali's smell. But I don't need my knowledge of the Vedas to remember what my own daughter smells like. The odor fills me with nostalgia for her, but I don't know why. Ray and my darling daughter never allowed us to have a normal family life. He was a ghost and she was a demon. I glance at Seymour. "This belongs to her."

He is not as happy as he was a moment ago. He may not remember the stake through his back, but he was there when Kalika opened Eric's throat. I carefully push the window back up and wipe away the faint impressions my palms have made on the glass.

"We'd better get out of here," he says.

I study the number at the front of the parking spot. "Eighteen twenty-one. It must be her suite number. We need to stake out this building."

"Not down here," he says quickly.

"No. We'll cross the street to the high-rise office building and find an empty office that has a view of the valet parking area. When she leaves, I'll break into her condo and search it."

He swallows. "Do we have to do that?"

"You don't have to do anything. I'll do it."

"But then you'll think I'm a coward."

"I know you're a coward," I lie.

He is insulted. "Is that why you won't sleep with me?"

"No. It's because you're still a nerd. Let's get across the street."

Back outside we cross Olympic Boulevard and enter one of the triangular towers that overlooks the condo towers. This commercial building has forty floors, twice what the condo towers have. A glance at the office listings in the main lobby tells me that 3450 and 3670 and 3810 and 2520 are empty. I steer Seymour toward the elevator. We are alone as we rise up to the thirty-sixth floor.

"Maybe she never goes out," he says. "We could wait all day for her to leave."

"You're free to go to a movie if you like."

"That's not fair. You're a vampire. You don't have to fear her the way I do."

"You will recall that last time I tried to attack her on the Santa Monica Pier, she grabbed my foot before I could touch her and snapped my ankle." I shake my head. "She can kill me as easily as she can kill you, if she chooses."

"But you do think a bullet in the head or in the heart will stop her?"

"Who really knows?"

Suite 3670 appears empty. I listen at the door for a moment before breaking the lock, stepping inside, and closing the door behind us. Suite 3670 directly overlooks the condo towers. We have a clear view of the valet area. If Kalika comes down and asks for her car, or simply gets it herself, we will know. Briefly I scan the portion of the eighteenth floor that faces us. It is possible I can see 1821, but I can't tell without examining the interior of the building or seeing a floor plan. Yet all of the condos on that floor have closed vertical blinds, so even if I was staring directly at her place, it would do me little good.

Seymour and I sit down on the floor and take up

the watch. Actually, it is only my eyes that are of any use. This high up, Seymour wouldn't recognize his own mother if she came out of the building across the street.

An hour goes by. Seymour gets hungry and goes for a sandwich. While he is gone I see a beautiful young woman with long dark hair come out of the condo tower. She hands the parking valet a dollar after he brings up her shiny white Mercedes. I am staring at the Dark Mother, the scourge of Suzama's prophecies, my own daughter.

"Kalika," I whisper to the glass. "What do you want?"

She climbs into her car and drives away. I am out the door in a flash. I run into Seymour on his way back with a sandwich for me. One look at my face and he is a mass of nerves. I raise my hand.

"I want you to stay here," I say. "I'm going into her condo, and you'll just get in my way."

"But you'll need a lookout," he protests.

"No."

"But I can't stay behind and let you take all the risks."

I decide not to be too quick to crush his brave initiative. Also, I am not in the mood to argue.

"All right," I say. "But if she rips your head off don't blame me."

He throws the sandwich in the garbage and we grab an elevator.

This time, at the condo tower, I have to speak to the receptionist, but I purposely keep the conversation short and silent. Catching her eye through the glass, I press her with my fiery will and mouth the words: *"Open the door."*

A moment later the door swings open.

Suite 1821 is naturally on the eighteenth floor. I do not want to break the lock because I still hope Kalika will know nothing of my visit. With a couple of pins I have brought for just this purpose, I quickly pick the lock. The door creaks open. Seymour stands behind me, the color of a hospital bed sheet.

"It's more fun to write about this stuff than do it," he says.

"Shh," I say as we step inside and close the door. "Stand on the front balcony and keep a lookout for her white Mercedes."

"What are you going to do?"

"Look for evidence of her state of mind."

Kalika owns, or rents, a two-bedroom corner condo. She has twin balconies and glorious views of the city. The place is elegant, the plush carpeting new, the white paint fresh. Her furnishings are few but tasteful. She seems to prefer traditional to modern, but nothing she has is old-fashioned. There are no magazines in the living room or dining area, yet she has a rather large TV, and I wonder how many channels she subscribes to and what her favorite programs are.

While Seymour stands outside on the balcony, I step into her office, the first bedroom on the right. She has a desk, a computer, a fax machine. Her drawers are unlocked and I rifle through them. Not entirely surprisingly, I find several maps. Most of them are of California, blow-ups of Big Sur, Mount Shasta, and Lake Tahoe. She has travel books on these areas also. There is also a guidebook on Sedona, which is located in Arizona. In another drawer are more books on these same places, but these are not typical travel guides. They contain personal accounts of the spots. I scan the books—I can read over thirty thousand words a minute with total comprehension. Quite a few of the stories describe how powerful the *vibrations* are in each place. I am fascinated because Kalika appears to be doing a lot of research on spots that have been New Age retreats for the last couple of decades.

"Do you like these places?" I whisper to myself. "Or do you think the child will be drawn to them?"

I move into my daughter's bedroom. Her queen-size bed is neatly made, covered with a hand-made quilt from China. In the corner, on top of a chest of drawers, a white silk cloth has been spread, almost as if a small altar has been set up. There are only a few books and a small Shiva Lingam set beside a brass incense holder in which a stick of musk incense has recently been burned.

The lingam is a polished gray phallic-shaped stone with three red marks on it. The shape and the markings are natural to the stone, I know. When I was a child, still a mortal, five thousand years ago, our tiny village had a Shiva Lingam. The rocks are supposed to contain the energy of Lord Shiva himself, Mahakala, who is the spouse of Mother Kali and the supposed destroyer of time at the end of all ages. Geologists describe lingams as the offspring of meteor crashes. In either case, they are highly magnetic. Brushing my hand over the stone, I feel its charge.

Kalika has three books beside the lingam: the *Bhagavad-Gita:* the *Upanishads,* the *Mahanirvana Tantra.* The Gita is the gospel according to Krishna, the *Upanishads* are collected stories of divine knowledge from ancient rishis, and the *Mahanirvana Tantra* describes Kali in her different avatars, and details her various modes of worship and innovation. All this reading material is entirely spiritual in nature. But try as I might, I cannot understand what that means. If I should be relieved or frightened. It is an old and regrettable truth that more people have been killed in the name of God than anything else.

I am picking up her copy of the *Gita* when Seymour bursts breathlessly into the room. "Her car just drove up," he says. "She wasn't gone long."

I replace the book in its exact spot. "It will take her a minute to get up here. Come, we have time."

Back out in the hallway, however, standing in front of the elevators, I begin to have doubts. As Seymour starts to push the down button, I stop him.

"Even in the garage basement," I say, "she might note the elevator going up to the eighteenth floor. She is shrewd—she might consider that more than coincidence." I pause. "Let's take the stairs."

"I just want to get out of here," Seymour says with emotion.

Halfway down the stairs I stop Seymour. Straining my ears to listen far below, I hear someone climbing up the stairs. The person is in no hurry and it could be anybody. But I don't like the fact that this person stands in our path, and that I can't see who it is—each floor is partitioned off. Seymour watches me anxiously.

"What is it?"

"Someone's coming up the stairs."

"Is it she?" he gasps.

"I can't tell." I pause. "I think it is a woman. This person has a light step."

"Oh God."

"Shh. She is far below still. Let's grab the elevator."

In the elevator, Seymour starts to push the button for the lobby, but I stop him for the second time and push the button for the second garage level. Seymour throws a fit.

"Why did you do that?" he asks.

"It is the last thing she'll expect us to do, if she thinks we know where her car is parked."

"But for all we know she's still in her car."

"Relax, Seymour. I know what I'm doing."

I hope. When the elevator *whooshes* open, I am tensed for an attack. But none comes. We appear to be alone in the underground garage. Signaling for Seymour to remain where he is, I step lightly into the garage and stretch my sensitive senses to their limits. There is no sign of Kalika. I signal to Seymour to join me.

"Let's just get our car and get out of here," I whisper in his ear.

He nods vigorously. "I am not cut out for this crap."

8

I call Dr. Seter in San Francisco but end up speaking to James, who acts happy to hear my voice. Perhaps it is not an act, but he does want to know if I am ready to show them my scripture. I tell him I have something even more important to show him. After making an appointment to see him and his father at the Hilton, after the lecture, I book a flight for San Francisco. As the plane lifts off the ground, Seymour nods to the manila envelope in my hand.

"What's that?" he asks.

"Newspaper clippings. Proof."

"I won't ask."

"You'll see soon enough."

We do not attend the lecture because I have a slight fear that Kalika will be there. We are waiting in the lounge area of the Hilton when Dr. Seter returns to the hotel. The elderly doctor looks fatigued from his travels and lecture, but James is as bright faced as ever. I introduce Seymour as an old friend and they take seats across from us. Dr. Seter orders a scotch and James a Coke. Seymour munches on the pretzels and sips cranberry juice.

I have nothing to eat or drink, not even a few drops of blood. I fear there may soon be enough blood flying to satisfy my most perverse thirsts. I wonder if Kalika still kills her victims, how many she hunts a night.

Dr. Seter studies me with tired eyes. For the first time I listen to his heart beat in his chest. He has clogged arteries, cardiac arrhythmia. He must know—I sense he is experiencing a tightness in his chest even now. Yet he smiles warmly before he begins to speak. He is a charming man.

"James tells me you have something exciting to show us," he says.

I stare at both of them for a moment.

"I know where the Dark Mother is," I say. "I need your help to kill her."

This gets their attention. Dr. Seter takes a moment to catch his breath. James glances at him anxiously, but I don't know if his anxiety is concern for his father's health or concern for the confrontation. Finally the doctor manages to speak.

"How do you know about the Dark Mother?" he

asks. "You said your scripture did not speak of a particular danger to the child."

"It speaks of her in general terms," I say. "And I know this young woman." I open the manila envelope I have brought with me. "I have chronicled her behavior. But perhaps you have as well. She's been in the papers lately."

First I give them clips from the *Los Angeles Times* of the series of brutal murders that were committed last December. Crazy Eddie Fender and his gang of nasty vampires were responsible for these crimes, but the murders are of such a bizarre nature—heads torn off, bodies drained of their blood—that I feel they strengthen my case. Next I show them clippings of the major shoot-out the police had with a gang of terrorists in downtown L.A.: three helicopters downed and dozens of police killed by a tiny but invincible force. Of course, I was responsible for those deaths. The police and FBI had the bad judgment to chase after me and Joel for our vampire blood.

I show them clippings of the Nevada nuclear explosion, and finally give them articles on Eric Hawkins, who was kidnapped from the park while playing basketball with friends. He was not found until weeks later, his throat scissored open by what appeared to be sharp fingernails. Yes, the words of the city coroner have made it all the way into the article, and they are surprisingly accurate. Naturally, it is only this last death Kalika was responsible for but now is not the time to reveal that. Dr. Seter and his son study the clippings for several minutes and then the doctor frowns at me.

"I don't see what this has to do with the Dark Mother," he says.

His voice is without conviction. I suspect that either he or James has been collecting similar clippings. The possibility strengthens my position and I decide to hold nothing back. I lean forward slightly as I speak and my tone is deadly serious.

"The Dark Mother is vampiric in nature," I say. "The original serial murders in L.A. all bear a vampiric stamp. This is when the Dark Mother moved into the Los Angeles area. Notice the dates of the murders, how they cease right after the terrorist shoot-out with the police. Yet these terrorists have never been found, never been identified. The media says it's because they escaped, but the real reason is that these terrorists never existed. In fact, the only one the police ever spoke about definitively was a young woman who was able to move extremely fast."

"We have read about her," James says, glancing at his father.

"Then there is the nuclear explosion in the Nevada desert," I continue. "Once again the media and the government drew a connection to terrorists, but here, too, they failed to identify the terrorists. Because there weren't any. For a brief time the Dark Mother was a prisoner of the military camp where the explosion occurred. But even with all their guns, all their tanks and soldiers, they couldn't contain her and she broke free and destroyed them. She went underground after that, yet she didn't leave the Los Angeles area. Note the description of Eric Hawkins's supposed kidnapper and compare it to the descriptions the police gave of the young woman who helped mess up downtown L.A. You will see they match. That's because all these events originate with one young woman who is not really a human being at all." I pause. "I know her name. I know where she lives. She may know I know this, I'm not sure. She won't remain where she is long. If you want to destroy her, you'll have to strike at her tonight. And don't look so shocked. I know you've prepared for a long time to do exactly this."

Dr. Seter is so taken aback by my words he can't speak. James takes up his role. "How do you know these things?" he asks. "You didn't read about them in an ancient scripture."

"I had a friend in the FBI who leaked parts of this information to me. He came to me originally because his agency was researching the Suzama material. This friend is now deceased—he died in the Nevada explosion. But before he died he gave me enough clues to locate and speak to the Dark Mother."

They both almost fall off their chairs. "You have seen her?" Dr. Seter exclaims.

"I have, too," Seymour says on cue. "We both spoke to her at the end of the Santa Monica Pier three months ago. She almost killed us both, but in the end decided to let us go."

"Why would she let you go if you're a danger to her?" Dr. Seter asks.

"She obviously doesn't think we are a danger to

her," I say. "Or else she thinks we may eventually lead her to the child. That's why she agreed to meet us, to quiz us about the Suzama material."

"We still need to see your scripture," Dr. Seter says.

"You can't," I say. "She destroyed it this afternoon. Furthermore, she might be on the verge of destroying your copy, along with the rest of you." I pause. "She was at your lecture last night."

James's voice is harsh. "Why didn't you tell us?"

"I didn't know," I say honestly. "I only found out today when she called me at home to tell me."

"Why would she call you?" Dr. Seter asks.

"I told you. I think she stays in touch because we—Seymour and I—might possibly lead her to the child. Plus you do not know her the way we do. To you she is just a name. To us she is a witch, who calls to taunt us, to let us know we live in her shadow."

Dr. Seter regards me critically. "What is her name? Do you know?"

"If I tell you, will you believe me?" I ask.

"Not necessarily," Dr. Seter says. "But I will at least give more credence to your wild story."

"Her name is Kalika, Kali Ma. This dark age of Kali Yuga is named after her."

Clearly Kalika is mentioned in Suzama's scripture. Their suddenly shocked expressions confirm this fact. Yet the information fills me with dismay. Is there no hope for my daughter? I know I am here to solicit aid in killing her but a part of me still longs to discover that I have made a terrible mistake, that all the horrors Kalika has committed since she drew her first breath are nothing more than misunderstandings. But it is not to be and I know it. Either my daughter dies or we do, and then also the child who can save the whole world. Dr. Seter is again having trouble catching his breath.

"Can this be true?" he whispers to himself.

"It is true," Seymour says. "I have seen with my own eyes what she can do. She is stronger than two dozen men combined, as fast as lightning. She is already stalking your group. You don't have much time."

James stares at Seymour. "How do you know Alisa?"

Seymour shrugs. "We're old friends."

James turns to me. "Neither of you has ever given us a last name. We have no way to check your background. We still don't know if you're with the government or not."

"The names we have given you are false," I say. "So what is the point in giving you a false last name? Surely you can understand our reasons for secrecy. We can talk all night and into the next morning. There is only one way of convincing you that we have found the Dark Mother, and that is to bring you to her. But when you do meet her, you have to be ready to kill her or else to be killed by her. It is that simple. You lose nothing by trusting me enough to check her out. Once again, that is if you have all your forces standing at full readiness."

Dr. Seter scoffs. "We don't have any forces."

"You are a poor liar, doctor," I say. "The FBI knows about your training exercises and your automatic weapons. They didn't interfere with you because there were agents, like my friend, who knew about the Suzama material and understood what you were preparing for. But those agents are dead now. Kalika killed them. As a result your group is threatened from all sides, politically and spiritually. You might even think I'm a threat, that I've been sent here by the Black Mother to lure you into a trap. Actually, there may be a particle of truth in that. I am not working for her, but if you do choose to confront her you may be wiped out. Seymour is not exaggerating her strength. But at least if you hit first you stand a chance. If you go after her you must hold back nothing. Yet you must first explain to your people what the real nature of the risk is. Tell them that several dozen police and marines couldn't stop her."

Dr. Seter is shaking his head. "This is all happening too fast. We can't do anything tonight. It's out of the question."

I don't want to push him, to fry his brain, or even to confuse his mind. I want the decision to be his because I suspect I am not exaggerating when I say many of his people may die. So I assuage my conscience. Yet I cannot let him stall. I feel he is close to agreeing with me. I have told him much that only he would know is true. It doesn't matter to me that I have lied to him a lot as well.

"You knew when the time came there would be no time for hesitation," I say gently. "She is down in Los Angeles, right now, in a condo with a wonderful view of the city. We were in her place this afternoon."

"She told you where she lives?" James asks.

"No. She made a mistake when she called me. That is all I can say. Seymour and I were then able to figure out where she lives."

"You traced her call?" James persists.

"In a manner of speaking," I say. "Dr. Seter, this is all real. I know you have been talking about it so long that it has lost some of its reality to you. But you only have to come with me tonight and bring your group, and you will see a five-thousand-year-old prophecy fulfilled before your very eyes."

He looks at me. "You are not a normal young woman, Alisa. There is something in your face, in your voice, in your eyes. James mentioned it last night and now I see it." He pauses. "How do we know you're not the Dark Mother?"

I smile sadly. "Some nights I feel as if I am. And even if I were, then that's all the more reason to heed my warning." Reaching over, I touch his knees. "Trust the inner senses that Suzama's material has given you. Trust what they are telling you right now." I pause. "Your whole life has led up to this moment."

Dr. Seter flashes a faint smile. "Somehow I can't imagine you are evil." He turns to James. "I need to talk to my son, alone, for a few minutes, if you please."

I stand and point to the entrance. "We will wait over there. We will give you all the privacy and time you need to decide."

Of course the moment we leave I stand still and listen to every word they say. It is a short but intense conversation.

James: "She knew the name of the Dark Mother! No one in our group except us knows that!"

Dr. Seter: "She knows many things I would have thought impossible. But that doesn't mean we can trust her."

James: "But you heard her argument. It's the same argument I've been giving you for the last few months. Those incidents we read about were all caused by a single deadly force. Only she has put the pieces together much better than we did. I'm telling you, father, I believe her. I say we throw everything we've got behind her."

Dr. Seter: "But just last night you were worried she was working for the Dark Mother."

James: "She is not behaving like someone who is trying to harm us. Right now she gave us a ton of information she didn't have to. Information that could be used against the Dark Mother."

Dr. Seter: "Only if it's true."

James: "It is true! Look, she only asks us to trust her so far. We will know within seconds of meeting this person if she is the Dark Mother. But she is right, we must be prepared for a major attack. It is the only way to protect our people."

Dr. Seter: "But what if she's lying to us? If she's working for the government and is trying to trap our group while it is engaged in illegal activities? Think about it, Jim, we're going to be storming a residence of some kind. If it is a government trap, we'll look like just another evil and confused cult in the eyes of the public."

James: "We'll have her with us when we make our attack. If she's lied to us, she'll pay the price."

Dr. Seter: "That's just talk. You wouldn't hurt her."

James: "I don't think I'll have to hurt her. I think our enemy will be so evil our hatred will be turned totally on her." A pause. "Let's do it. If we don't, Father, we will regret it for the rest of our lives. That's what my inner feelings tell me."

Dr. Seter is a long time answering. But finally he gives his OK.

9

The attack has yet to begin but already I realize something is very strange. I had initially gone to Dr. Seter and James because I knew I was physically and emotionally ill-equipped to kill Kalika. She is too strong for me, and I can't imagine hurting her. All I wanted to do was send in twenty people with guns, close my eyes, and be told it was all over. Your daughter is dead, the world is safe for democracy again. Yet the Suzama Society seems to be much more than twenty people with guns. It should reassure me that they are better prepared than I imagined, yet it does not, and I puzzle over this.

I stand in Suite 3670, in the commercial building

across the street from Kalika's condo tower. Olympic Boulevard lies between us and my daughter, but at this time of night—three in the morning—it is rare that a car drives by. Beside me are Dr. Seter, Seymour, James, and two sharpshooters with laser-assisted rifles. They have cut away a circular panel in the glass and now are focusing their weapons on Kalika's windows, which are visible, barely—for we are eighteen stories above her. All of Kalika's windows are covered with vertical blinds, however. We have better views of her two balconies and the large pool far below. Of course, we have a clear view of the roof of the tower. It is at this spot that I stare as my doubts continue to grow.

Dr. Seter and his son have not assembled a group of spiritual fanatics and trained them how to aim and fire automatic weapons. Instead they have managed to construct the equivalent of a highly trained commando unit. I am staggered by the way they go about surrounding Kalika, who, by the way, is definitely at home. Their attack is much more coordinated than the attack the LAPD and the FBI sprang to capture me and Joel.

There are two units: Alpha Top and Alpha Bottom. The former has somehow managed to make it onto the roof of the building with ropes and pulleys. Alpha Bottom is already on Kalika's floor. The security guards are apparently unconscious, if we are to believe the radio reports that are constantly streaming in. We're all tied together with short wave. Both Alpha Top and Alpha Bottom have ten members each, male and female, all dressed in black. They have night goggles, gas grenades, even grenade launchers. Where they bought all this stuff, I have no idea.

I watch as the last of the Alpha Top team assembles on the roof.

"How do they plan on getting down to Kalika's balcony?" I ask James, pointing at the people on the roof. James is also dressed in black, a radio in his hand. His face shines with excitement. Apparently he likes playing soldier. The whole situation strikes me as odd, and yet I am the one who instigated it—I think.

"The same way they got on the roof," he says. "We will lower six of them onto the balconies before we attack, three onto each balcony. We won't attack until everyone is in position. Why?"

"She will hear them on the balcony," I say.

James peers through a pair of binoculars hung around his neck. "We have pretty much determined that she is asleep."

"I wouldn't count on that," Seymour mutters.

"We must give her a chance to cooperate," Dr. Seter says for perhaps the tenth time. Although the doctor is supposed to be the boss, it is clear to me the attack units are taking orders only from James.

"She'll be given every chance she deserves," James says. He clicks on his radio. "Alpha Bottom, this is Control. Are you still holding by the eighteenth floor elevators? Over."

"Control, this is Alpha Bottom. We are near the elevators. Over."

"Alpha Bottom, this is Control. Alpha Top will be swinging onto the balconies momentarily. Do not move toward Suite Eighteen Twenty-one until you are ordered. Over."

"Control, this is Alpha Bottom. Understood. Out."

James studies the top group through his binoculars. Then he clicks his radio back on. "Alpha Top, this is Control. Any signs that Kalika is in the living room or kitchen area? Over."

"Control, this is Alpha Top. We have detected no activity in the living room or kitchen area. Over."

"Alpha Top, are your ropes in place? Over."

"Control, we are ready to swing down. Over."

"Alpha Top, this is Control. You may start down. But hold on the balconies until you hear from me. Over."

"Control, understood. Alpha Top out."

"You guys seem to know what you're doing," I say.

James smiles. "You sound disappointed."

I give a wan smile. "I always have a thing for the underdog." More than a thing. Watching them all converge on Kalika, I feel sick to my stomach. I have to keep telling myself that Kalika is totally unpredictable, that they have to be careful. Dr. Seter puts a hand on my arm.

"We have trained for this day for a long time," he says. "But we will not shoot first, I promise you that. She will be given every chance to surrender."

I shake my head. "She will never surrender."

In teams of three, dropping off from two points on the roof, the Alpha Top people begin to slide down toward the balconies. They land in seconds;

I watch as they unclip the ropes from their belts. Each carries a weapon, has a radio in an ear, and night goggles. The guy in charge of Alpha Top comes back on the line, speaking in hushed whispers.

"Control, we are in position. Over."

"He shouldn't be talking," I say. "She'll hear him. In fact, they should be ready for her to attack. Now. Tell them to get their weapons drawn. She could come at them any second."

James ignores me. He talks into his radio.

"Alpha Top, this is Control. You will go on my command. Stand ready. Over."

Separated by a corner of the building, neither group of three can see the other group. This is a major weakness in the plan. They should know to the split second what every one of them is doing. Their radios are not fast enough. James continues to bark instructions.

"Alpha Bottom, this is Control. Move toward Suite Eighteen Twenty-one. Alpha Top is in position on the balconies. Over."

"Control, this is Alpha Bottom. Understood. Over."

The ten people on the Alpha Bottom team will crowd one another as they move along the hallway. I point this out to James and suggest he hold back half of them by the elevators. He brushes aside my comment.

"They know what they're doing," he says. "They won't accidentally shoot each other."

"You don't understand how fast she can move,"

I say. "The more room they have, the more chance they have of getting off a clean shot."

"I want Alpha Bottom to knock at the door first," Dr. Seter says. "She has to be told that she is surrounded and that escape is impossible."

"She doesn't think in terms of impossibilities," Seymour mutters. "I think it will be a mistake to knock."

James checks with me. "Do you agree?"

I think of Kalika riddled with bullets while she lies in bed.

"I agree." I turn to Dr. Seter. "There is no point in talking to her. Honestly."

Dr. Seter trembles. "But this could be cold-blooded murder."

"I say we listen to Alisa," James says. Before anyone can protest he clicks on his radio. "Alpha Top and Alpha Bottom, this is Control. We will move on the count of five. One . . . two . . . three . . ."

He does not reach five.

There is loud screaming.

We hear it over the radio and through the air.

We look down to see that the balcony farthest from us is empty—of Suzama people, that is. Kalika, alone, is out there, her hair hanging down the back of her white robe. Below her, three individuals in black float down toward the large swimming pool. Float is perhaps too kind a word. They are falling to their deaths, and they know it. The few feet of pool water are not going to absorb their falls. Their horrified screams rend the air and I scream at myself for believing that Kalika would just lie down and die.

The three hit the water, landing on top of each other, crashing through to the bottom. Their limbs and skulls explode on contact. The pool is well lit. Within seconds a red wave expands across the blue water. The screams cease. I turn to James.

"Call off the attack!" I yell. "Get your people out of there! She may let them go if they pull back now!"

James stares down in horror as blood fills the pool.

"This is incredible," he mumbles.

I grab him. "I was wrong! She can't be stopped this way! Tell them to back off!"

He looks at me and frowns. "No. We have only started to fight." He touches his two sharpshooters on the shoulders, the two that crouch below us. "Open fire."

Their bullets begin to ricochet off the balcony. Kalika moves inside.

"Alpha Top!" James shouts into his radio. "She is coming."

No, she has come. Before James can finish speaking, Kalika attacks those on the second balcony. Only my eyes are fast enough to see exactly what she does. The person closest to the balcony door is a woman with long red hair. Kalika grabs her and twists her head all the way around. Catching the dead woman's weapon as it falls, Kalika then shoots the other two in the face. One, a handsome guy with no top skull, falls over the balcony and lands on the sidewalk seventeen floors below. The third one, a short dark guy, simply sits down and dies. Before our sharpshooters can readjust their aim to the nearer balcony, Kalika has retreated inside. And now she has an automatic weapon with her. James struggles to turn his radio back on.

"Alpha Bottom!" he yells. "You must attack!"

"What has happened to Alpha Top?" the guy wants to know.

"Those on the balcony have been taken out!" James says and forgets all the "Alpha" this and "over" that. There is no time for such formalities. "She is still inside! Get her!"

"Tell them she has a gun!" I say.

"She has a gun!" James yells. "Alpha Top, you must get down to the balconies! Alpha Bottom is going in!"

The four still on the roof are peering over the edges. They see that the pool is full of bodies and so is one of the balconies. Why, there is even a body down on the sidewalk. They don't want to go anywhere. I wish they would go back the way they came. I know they are in extreme danger just by being on the roof.

"We have to stop!" Dr. Seter cries to his son, his face ashen. "Alisa is right! Don't send any more people."

The radio is screaming.

Now Alpha Bottom is dying.

They have kicked in her door, violated her space. There are gunshots, sounds of tearing flesh, splattering blood, breaking bones. And over it all I hear Kalika laughing. She is unstoppable and knows it. It is only then I realize that from the very beginning this has been a trap. Seymour was right. Kalika let me hear enough to figure out where she lived. She knew I would try to get help, and since she obviously doesn't like the Suzama group, so much the better that they should come to her to die. I hear one woman begging for mercy and then it sounds as if she is smashed against a wall. James trembles with the radio in his hand.

"Alpha Top!" he shouts. "Help your partners!"

The four still on the roof look at one another and shake their heads. They would be better off getting down from the roof, yet they must think they are safe up there because they hardly move while the screaming continues. But when it stops, and the firing stops, I finally grab the radio from James's hands.

"Alpha Top," I say calmly. "She knows you're up there. Try to go back down the way you came up. Don't wait for her to come to you. Please, listen to me. Swing down to the nineteenth floor and get in the elevator. There's still time."

But what time there is they squander. A precious minute elapses while they seem to argue among themselves. At the end of that time, Kalika, her white robe now soaked red, peeks over the edge of the roof. They see her, and those left of Alpha Top are too scared even to level their weapons. As Kalika climbs up onto the roof, they slowly back into the corner farthest from her. Even the sharp-shooters at our knees stare in awe. James slaps one on the head.

"Shoot her!" he shouts. "She's an easy target!"

But my daughter makes nothing easy. As a bullet

sparks at her feet, she leaps forward and grabs one of the men and holds him as a shield in front of her. The other three continue to stand immobilized by fear. But now Kalika is looking our way. The sharpshooters cease firing. James throws a tantrum.

"Don't stop!" he screams. "Kill her!"

"But she's holding Charles," one protests.

"Oh God, this can't be happening," Dr. Seter moans.

James shoves the guy aside. "Give me that gun!"

But I stop James. "Let me," I say quietly.

He glares at me. "What do you know about sniper rifles?"

"She knows a lot," Seymour says.

James continues to glare at me, but finally lets me take the gun.

"Just don't miss," he says bitterly.

Kneeling behind the stationary rifle, I peer into the telescopic sight. Kalika is standing relatively motionless, but she still has the guy held neatly in front of her. Only her face is visible behind the guy's right shoulder. The laser guide is helpful, even for someone like me who can hit a dime-size object at two miles if I have the right gun. For a moment I am able to plant the red dot precisely in the center of Kalika's forehead. My finger sweats over the trigger. I merely have to pull it and put a bullet in her brain and the night can still be considered a success, at least as far as the world is concerned.

But then I catch sight of her eyes, and I hesitate. She seems to be looking directly at me. Who am I fooling? Of course she knows who tracks her. The fact seems to amuse her because she smiles ever so faintly. Her lips move to form a soundless word, yet I hear it, hear it inside.

"Mother."

I momentarily lose my concentration. In that time Kalika moves swiftly and with deadly purpose, vanishing from the field of view of my laser scope. Pulling back from the weapon, I watch her throw her human shield off the side of the roof. She tosses her victim straight at the pool—perhaps it amuses her to see the big red splash the screaming people make—and a moment later there is that much more blood to clean out of the filter.

In quick succession she grabs two of the three who are left. These she kills by smashing their skulls together. They are unrecognizable as she lets them fall onto the rooftop, their brains hanging over their collars. Then her attention turns to the final member of the Suzama Society, and I recognize her. Lisa, the accountant from North Dakota, whom I met last night. So great is Lisa's fear that she backs away from my daughter, right off the side of the roof. Kalika does not let her fall, but grabs her at the last instant. James yells at me.

"Why don't you shoot!" he says.

I set the gun down. "No. I can't kill Lisa."

"Lisa is as good as dead!" James cries. "Shoot!"

But Kalika has already disappeared with her prey, a spider crawling back into her web with a kicking insect in tow. The roof is now empty except for two virtually headless bodies.

I stand and look at all of them. "Stay here. I am going to speak to her."

Dr. Seter grabs my arm. "You can't go over there, child. It's a bloodbath."

I gently remove his hand. "I am responsible for this." I turn to Seymour. "I have to go."

Seymour is devastated by my decision. "There's no point."

"That is probably the understatement of the year," I agree.

10 ~~~

The moment I am out the door I switch into hyper-mode. Using the stairs instead of waiting for the elevator, I reach the condo in less than one minute. In the distance I hear the cry of a dozen sirens. Yet the police are not really late to respond. Since the beginning of the attack less than seven minutes have elapsed. Kalika was definitely not sleeping.

Standing outside the building is a tide of moaning souls in pajamas and robes. Somebody should at least turn off the pool lights, I think. The floating bodies create a particularly gruesome sight. A few of the people, all men in their forties, have guns in their hands. They are arguing with one another as I dash inside the building.

I take the stairs to the eighteenth floor. Between the sixteenth and seventeenth floors I find two brutally slain bodies, their heads literally torn from their bodies.

"Would you be upset if I ripped this bird's head off?"

"Why do you ask these silly questions?"

"To hear your answers."

The sight of these poor people upsets me greatly, but it makes me pause to ask myself the question: what am I doing? Am I trying to save Lisa in order to bandage my shattered conscience for the other deaths I have caused? Not that Lisa is not worth my effort, but I know she is as James said, as good as dead. And if I die with her who will be left to stop Kalika?

But these questions, like most, are academic.

I hear cries above me. Lisa, in the claws of a jackal.

Picking up an automatic rifle, I continue up the stairs.

Kalika is waiting for me in the center of her living room. I have to walk over a glut of slashed bodies to get to her. The place is not as neat as it was that afternoon when Seymour and I investigated. There is hardly a square foot of wall or ceiling or floor that is not splattered red. Apparently my daughter let them come as far as they wanted into her home before she welcomed them as only she knows how.

Yet Lisa is still alive. In Kalika's arms.

I level my gun at the two of them.

"It's a coward who hides behind another," I say to my daughter.

Kalika smiles. Her face, her arms, even her hair are drenched in blood, and she has never looked happier. Tightening her hold on Lisa, she lifts the young woman a foot off the floor. For her part, Lisa is half in shock, with at least one foot in the grave. Yet she continues to struggle against my daughter, all the while making feeble whimpering sounds. The fight in her is instinctive. I believe Kalika has already shattered her mind.

"We did this once before," she says. "But you were not carrying a weapon that night."

"I am not going to put the gun down," I say.

Kalika chuckles. "Then I should kill her now?"

"No." I take a step forward. "Let her go. Show your mercy."

"Drop the gun. Show your courage."

"You will just kill us both."

"Perhaps," Kalika agrees.

"You set me up. You wanted me to bring them here. Why?"

"I would think the answer to that question is obvious."

"The police will be here in minutes," I say.

"The police do not concern me." She raises a sharp nail to Lisa's throat. "I cannot let you shoot me, Mother. I have a mission yet to perform."

"What is it?"

"To protect the righteous and to destroy the wicked."

I sneer. "Tonight is a fine example of that mission of yours."

"Thank you." Kalika presses her nail into Lisa's neck. A drop of blood appears and traces a line down the young woman's throat. Lisa, even though in shock, suddenly gasps and struggles harder. But Kalika's hold is stronger than steel. She speaks casually. "You remember this part, don't you, Mother?"

I begin to panic. I cannot let this girl die. She is almost a stranger to me, true, but she is all that Dr. Seter has left. If I can save her, I think, I can save the doctor. I know his heart will give out soon after this night. You will see prophecies fulfilled. Yeah, right. The Satanic Prophecies. How could I make him such promises? Kalika is right about one thing. I lie to suit my needs. It is an old habit of mine.

"You promised me this morning that you would not kill unless it was necessary," I say.

Kalika digs her nail in a little deeper. The red line on Lisa's throat thickens. Soon the blood will gush. Lisa's eyes are as round as overripe strawberries. Her breathing sounds labored. Or is that her heart I hear, skipping inside her trembling chest? Lisa is almost gone but still her expression begs for me to save her.

"This is becoming necessary," Kalika says. "Put down the gun."

"I can't."

"I will open her throat. She will go the way Eric did. You know how much that upset you."

Now I shake. "But this young woman is innocent."

"She came to kill me. Innocence is hardly the word I would apply to her."

"I brought her here. I am to blame. Please, Kalika, for the love of God, let her go."

Kalika pauses. "For the love of God? How can you say that to me after you have gazed into my eyes? Don't you know I do everything for the love of God?"

With that Kalika scratches her sharp nail all the way across Lisa's throat, opening two of the young woman's major arteries. The blood shoots out as if fired from a hose under tremendous pressure. But I am hardly given a chance to react, to fire through Lisa's body now that it has ceased to be a viable living shield. My daughter is swifter than Eddie Fender was. Lisa gags on pieces of throat as Kalika throws her at me. The blow is enough to knock me over and send my weapon flying. The back of my skull strikes a wall as Lisa slowly slips from me and everything is a blur to me for a moment. There is blood on the back of my own head. I reach up to feel the extent of my injury when I see a figure out of the corner of my eye. It is my daughter holding my gun. She speaks in a kind voice.

"Are you in pain?" she asks.

The room continues to spin. Lisa's body weighs heavily on my lower legs.

"Go to hell," I mumble.

"I am beyond heaven and hell." She reaches out and grabs my arm. "You have friends in the other building. Save me time and tell me what suite they're in."

Finally my eyes begin to refocus. I stare at her.

"You've got to be kidding," I say.

She smiles. "Just thought I would ask. Do you know how to swim?"

"Yes."

"Do you know how to fly?"

Sounds like a trick question to me.

I don't answer it but it doesn't matter.

Tossing aside the gun, Kalika grabs me by the chest and with one hand drags me outside and onto the balcony where she dealt with the first three members of Alpha Top. Far below the bodies continue to float in the red-stained pool. The police have finally arrived. Numerous black and white units are jammed into the valet parking area, their search beams pointed at us. I would wave but I'm afraid they might shoot me. Kalika sighs in wonder as she sweeps the city night with her dark eyes.

"I told you the view was stunning," she says.

"I am pleased that my only daughter should be so successful that she is able to afford such a nice place," I say sweetly.

Kalika leans over and kisses me on the cheek. Her lips are soft and gentle. She speaks in my ear and there is a trace of concern in her voice.

"Can you survive such a fall? Tell me the truth."

"I honestly don't know."

She pulls back slightly and strokes my hair. "Krishna loves you."

I am having trouble breathing. Her grip is cruel.

"It is good somebody does," I gasp.

"Did I ever tell you that I love you?"

"No. Not that I can remember."

"Oh." A deadly pause. "I must have forgotten."

"Kalika—"

I am not given a chance to finish the sentence.

My own daughter throws me over the side of the balcony.

The moon is out, it is true, and it is very bright. But there is no time to allow its gentle rays to pour into the crown of my head and fill my body to float me safely away as it did when the nuclear bomb threatened to kill me. At the moment I could be a mortal. Certainly I fall as fast as one. Kalika has thrown me toward the pool. As the bloody mess rushes toward me, I can only pray that I land in the deep end.

When I hit, my arms and legs are spread as far as they will go. I reason that this will give me more of a chance to break my fall. But I know even before I strike the water that something else will break when I strike the bottom of the pool.

The shock is crushing. There is a flash of red followed by an agony so searing I lose consciousness. But the oblivion is cruel; it does not last. When I awake my face is pressed into the floor of the pool. Indeed I have cracked the plaster, and half the bones in my body. My nose seems to have been obliterated, my face is a pancake of gross tissue. Inside my torn mouth I feel a lump of crumbled teeth. My chest feels as if ribs poke through my lungs and my shirt, pouring more blood into the pool.

Honestly, I don't think I can live through this.

Especially under nine feet of water.

The dead float above me, their expressionless

faces inviting me to join them. The water seems to swim with nightmarish creatures. One of my black boots floats by. My sock, covered in red, is still inside. My spinal cord is possessed by a pain demon. He has brought sharp tools. I throw up in the water and blood and teeth come out and form a ghastly cloud over my head. I start to lose consciousness again, and I know if I do, I will never wake up. Yet my eyes refuse to remain open. They are broken as well. Closing them, I sink into a deeper level of darkness.

Krishna. Let me have one more chance. That is all I ask.

To stop her. To save the child.

My heart keeps beating. The agony keeps throbbing.

Time goes by but pain counts it at a different speed. This time is what is called hard time by all those who have suffered. And hard times bring hard truths. My brains may be leaking from my ears, but I finally understand that Kalika cannot be defeated by guns and bullets. Twenty people, maybe more, had to die to make me understand that.

But I will never understand how she can be so cruel.

"But anyone who sees through the veil of maya cannot fathom the divine will. The veil is stained and the absolute is without flaw. One cannot reveal the other. In the same way, I am your own daughter but you cannot fathom me."

No matter how many die, I will not understand.

From far away, I feel feverish activity. It comes, I

realize, from deep inside me, in my muscles, beneath my veins, and all around my joints. My supernatural body is trying to knit itself back together. Beneath my shirt, I feel my sternum grow back together into one piece. Next there are pops in my legs and ankles. The bones are resetting themselves at a frantic pace. My jaw flexes involuntarily and I feel new teeth pressing up from beneath my mangled gums. Finally I am able to open my eyes, and I give myself a gentle push toward the surface. The beat of my heart has turned to a shriek. If I do not draw in a breath soon, especially with all the repair work going on, my chest will explode.

The night air tastes good. Never better.

On the surface, I am forced to float on my back for a minute before I am strong enough to make my way to the side. There is a crowd gathered, and some of the people in it are cops. I hear screams as I begin to pull myself out of the pool, but a brave cop rushes to my side with a clean blanket. He is fat with a bushy mustache. He carefully wraps the blanket around me.

"You're going to be OK," he says. "Just lie here on the deck. Don't try to move. You may have broken bones."

I wipe at the blood on my face. I know I don't have much time.

"You have friends in the other building."

"No, I'm fine," I say. "Don't worry about me."

I try to stand but he tries to stop me.

"But you were thrown off that balcony," he protests. "It's a miracle you're still alive."

I finish wiping my face and hair with his blanket

and hand it back to him all bloody. "You're a kind man," I say. "But I have to get out of here."

I move too fast for him to stop me—yet I am far from healed. Even as I dash across Olympic Boulevard, I feel the tissue inside my body struggling to recover. If I meet Kalika in the next minute I will be at a serious disadvantage. Not that it will make much difference. But it is fear that hurries me along, or maybe it is foolish hope. Hope that she might have let some of them survive.

In the office building, the elevator takes me to the thirty-sixth floor. The stairs are too much for me in my condition. When I stagger out of the elevator, the first thing I see is blood. For a moment all hope in me dies. The door to Suite 3670 has been pulverized. Yet there is a sound, soft words, faint moans. I hurry forward and peer inside.

Seymour and Dr. Seter huddle in one corner. My old friend appears to be taking care of the doctor, who's having trouble catching his breath. Twenty feet away from them, in the center of the room, the two sharpshooters lie in an ugly heap. It looks as if she kicked each of them so hard in the chest that she ruptured their hearts—an old Sita move. Yet Seymour and Dr. Seter appear unharmed. I almost weep I am so relieved.

It is only then I notice that James is missing.

"Where is he?" I demand.

They jump and look over. I am still covered with blood.

Dr. Seter gasps. "We thought you were dead."

I stride toward them and look down. "Where is James? Did she take him?"

Seymour stands and shakes his head. "He went after you, right after you left. We haven't seen him since." He hugs me; there are tears on his face. "Thank God you're alive. We saw her throw you off the balcony. I thought it was all over."

I comfort him, but also catch his eye. "That was someone else you saw. Not me." I turn back to the doctor. "You have a heart condition. Will you be all right? Should I call for an ambulance?"

"I'll be fine." He reaches up. "Just help me up."

I do so. "What happened?" I ask.

Seymour gestures weakly. "The door exploded and she walked in. The guys tried to shoot her, but she didn't give them a chance. Then she pinned Dr. Seter to the wall and demanded he tell her where the scripture was."

Dr. Seter looks crushed. "And I told her everything. I tried to resist but I couldn't." He stops and he is close to crying. "Do you think she got James?"

"No." The voice comes from the door. James steps into the room. He surveys the dead sharpshooters and a shudder goes through his body. "I am unharmed," he says.

I step to his side. "Did you see her leave?"

"Yes. She stole a cop car and drove away in it."

"Did you see anything else?"

I am asking if he saw me hit the pool and survive.

He stares at me. "No. I mean, what do you mean? It's a holocaust over there."

"Nothing. I am sorry about tonight," I say. "I know the words sound stupid but I must say them. At least now you can see why she must be stopped."

Placing my hand over his heart, as I had the previous night, I am surprised at how evenly it is beating. He got rattled during Kalika's attack but has quickly regained his cool. I add, "You have to show me the remainder of your scripture. If it is still there."

11 ～

Kalika was thorough. The Suzama Society has only two members now. The news shocks me. Surely, I say to James as he drives us toward Palm Springs, there have to be some personnel at the center who weren't involved in the attack.

"No," he replies. He adds with a bitter laugh, "We're all true believers. We believed your story, and went after the Dark Mother with everything we had." The morning sun is bright in his face but James appears close to despair as he thinks about the previous night. "We don't even have a secretary at the center now."

I reach over and rub his shoulders. "It wasn't

your fault. If anyone is to blame, it is I. I knew what she could do."

"But you did warn us. You warned me. If I had listened to your suggestions, maybe fewer would have been killed."

"No. It wouldn't have made any difference. She was determined to kill them all."

He frowns. "Why did she spare my father and your friend?"

"That puzzles me," I say honestly. "The only thing I can think is that she must believe that either your father or Seymour, working with us, will eventually find the child."

He is concerned. "Do you think she's following us now?"

I have been checking to see if we are being shadowed.

"Not at this very moment, no," I say.

"Do you think my father and your friend will be safe at your house?"

He is not asking about a threat from Kalika. We are all fugitives from the law now, from the government. I have no doubt my description has been relayed to those higherups who knew I was at the military base in Nevada. My face has shown up at too many public slaughters lately. There is an excellent chance, I think, that the police or the FBI will be waiting for us at the Suzama Center in Palm Springs. When the bodies are all identified, they will make the natural link. That's why I have insisted we go to the center immediately. I have yet to decide if I will kill to see the scripture.

"For the time being," I say. "Your father can rest there, and Seymour will take good care of him." I pause. "You worry about him, don't you?"

He nods. "His heart is lousy."

"Are you adopted?"

My question surprises him. "Yes. I was adopted late. I was sixteen when my parents were killed in a car accident. At the time Dr. Seter and my father were colleagues at Stanford. He started out watching me so I started calling him dad, at first only as a joke. But now I feel closer to him than I did to my real father. A short time after I moved in with him he found the scripture and then we shared a mission together as well as a house."

"Where did he find it?"

He hesitates. "Israel. In Jerusalem."

"That's not Western Europe."

"It's better if he's not specific. Where did you find yours? Tell me the truth this time."

"In Jerusalem."

He nods. "And Kalika destroyed it yesterday?"

"She took it. I don't know if she destroyed it."

"So she lets you live as well."

"I suppose," I say, feeling sad. My own daughter tried to kill me. And there had been a time not so long ago when I was willing to risk losing the world to save her. Now I see I have lost my bet, even though I am still angling for another chance to win back what has been lost. I wonder if Krishna heard my prayer while I lay on the bottom of the pool, if he let me live for a reason. I wonder if Paula's child is Krishna.

From the outside the center appears to be undisturbed, but once we are in the basement it is clear that someone has been in the vault. Sheets of the scripture lie spread on the table in the center of the room. James grabs them frantically and studies them. The color drains from his face.

"She was here," he says. "Some papyrus sheets are missing. Others are torn in pieces."

His conclusion seems logical, yet I can find no trace of her smell in the basement, and that puzzles me.

"Are you sure there are no other members of the Suzama Society alive?" I ask.

"There are just me and my dad," he says.

I stop him. "Go upstairs and keep watch. Let me try to read what is here."

"But less than half of it is here."

I realize his whole adult life has been built around the document. Giving him a comforting pat on the back, I shoo him away. Finally I am alone with a piece of the puzzle I have never held before. But I have to wonder about what is missing.

The first piece I read deals specifically with the child.

Of all the previous avatars, he who is born at the end of that time's millennium will manifest the greatest divinity to the world. He will have the playfulness of Sri Krishna, the wisdom of Adi Shankara, and the compassion of Jesus of Nazareth. He will be these divine beings, but something more, something that humanity has never seen before.

He will be born in a city associated with lost

angels, but it will be dark angels who force him and his mother to flee to the mirror in the sky, where shoes move without feet and the emerald circle is seen in the morning light. There the dark forces will once again converge on him, but a powerful angel will rescue him only to lose him again. Then the place of sanctity will be defiled by red stars, and only the innocent will see the blue light of heaven. Faith is stronger than stone. The rest is a mystery.

The war between the Setians and the Old Ones never ends. I am Suzama of the Old Order. Even as these words are recorded, the mother of an angel burns under Setian stars. Her pain is my pain. I wait for the enemy, for the splinter in the earth element, and for my own death. This splinter will become a crack, and civilization will end as we know it. But all ends are temporary and all life is born from death. I am Suzama and I fear neither this end nor the loss of my own life. For this ancient war is for the purpose of dark angels and blue angels alike. Both are divine in my illumined vision, and all color is erased in the infinite abyss.

There is another piece of papyrus, torn in two. It is much thinner than the others. It speaks of Kalika.

She is the Dark Mother, all consuming and not to be trusted. She brings the light of the red stars, and a wave of red death flows from her fingertips. She is the scourge of the child, not its protector as she claims to be. Her name is Kali

Ma, and it is her name that matches the dark age. All who know her will fear her.

"Suzama," I whisper, shaking. "You don't know how you curse your old friend."

But does it matter what she says about my daughter? Wasn't tonight proof enough of my daughter's demonic nature? She laughed as she killed, and no doubt drank the blood of many of those who slumped to their deaths. Suzama can tell me nothing new about my own child.

But what about the holy child? Where is this mirror in the sky, where shoes move without feet and the emerald circle is seen in the morning light? It is difficult to imagine Suzama being any more ambiguous. I almost curse her. The last thing I need now is more riddles, and all the stuff about dark angels and mistaken angels confuses me. Even worse are Suzama's references to the Setians. They were destroyed when Suzama was destroyed, in the great earthquake of ancient Egypt. Why does she go on about the war? That war is over as far as I am concerned.

"I will wait here for you. I will be here when you return."

But there was no one there when I returned.

Suzama's last prediction to me was wrong.

I call to James and he returns to the basement quickly.

"There are people outside on the street pointing at the center," he says. "I think the police will be here any minute."

"We will go then. Gather up what is left of the scripture and take it to your father."

"Aren't you going with me?" he asks.

"No. I need some time alone to think. Do you have an extra car?"

He grimaces. "We have plenty of extra cars now. You can take any one you want. Should I go to your house?"

"Yes. I will join you there shortly. Go out the back way so you won't be stopped."

He is dying to ask the question.

"Did you find out anything useful?" he asks.

I give a wan smile. "Only time will tell."

12 ~

On the spot where Paula's child was conceived, on the sandy bluff in Joshua Tree National Monument, I lie in the shade of a tall Joshua tree and stare up at the sky. It strikes me as a small miracle how the sky has not changed in five thousand years. Why, I could be lying on my back in ancient Egypt, beside the Nile, and there would be no difference in the sky.

But it is not easy for me to remember.

Suzama took me in, into her home, her heart. She shared a small shack with her parents. It is ironic that the greatest seer of all time should be born to a blind mother and a blind father. Neither of them ever knew what I looked like, yet they treated me with great kindness. They even tolerated the strange hours I kept. For in those days I needed to drink blood almost every night to quench my thirst. It was still difficult for me to feed myself and keep my victim alive. I lacked the control that was to come with age. Yet many people naturally died in those days during the night, especially the old, and I tried to confine my feeding to them so as to raise fewer suspicions.

When I returned home from one nightly sojourn, I found Suzama awake. At that time I had been in Egypt a month. There was pain in Suzama's large soulful eyes. She sat outside beneath a blanket of stars. I sat beside her.

"What's the matter?" I asked.

She would not look at me. "I followed you tonight."

I drew in a sharp breath. "What did you see?"

"What you do to people." She had tears. "Why do you do it?"

I took a while to answer her. "I have to do it to survive."

It was true. She of almost perfect clairvoyance could not see what her friend really was. When she had first met me, she had only suspected.

She was horrified. "Why?"

"Because I am not a human being. I am a vampire."

Even in those days they had a word for creatures like me. Suzama understood what I meant. Yet she did not flee from me, but instead held my hand.

"Tell me how it happened," she said.

I told her the entire story of my life, which even

though it had just begun, seemed awfully long to me. Suzama heard of Yaksha and Rama and Lalita and Krishna. I told her every word Krishna had said to me, of the vow he had placed me under to make no more vampires, and of the vow he had made Yaksha take to destroy all vampires. Suzama listened as if in a dream. When I was finished she whispered aloud.

"I have seen this Krishna in many visions," she said.

"Tell me what you see?"

She spoke in a distant voice. "He has the whole universe in his eyes. The sun we see in the sky is only one of many. All these stars—more than can be counted—shine inside the crown of his head." She paused. "You must be a very special kind of monster to receive his grace."

I was able to relax.

Suzama was telling me she was still my friend.

It was shortly after that night that she began to heal others.

The cures started innocently enough. Suzama was fond of collecting herbs. Even as a child she had had a knack for knowing which ones to prescribe for which illnesses. It was normal for a handful of ailing people to stop by each day for medical advice. Sometimes Suzama would have the sick person stay. She would have the person lie on his or her back and take long, slow deep breaths while she held her left hand above the forehead and her right hand over the heart. Invariably the person felt better afterward, or at least they said they did.

Then came a crippled man. He had not walked

since a massive stone had fallen across his hips five years earlier. He had no feeling from the waist down. At first she prescribed some herbs and was about to send him away when the man begged her to bless him. Reluctantly, as if she knew this act would forever change the course of her life, Suzama put him down on the floor and had him take deep breaths. Her hands shook as she held them over the man, and there was sweat on her face. I couldn't take my eyes off her. A milky white radiance had begun to shine above her head. Even when the man's lower legs began to twitch, I couldn't stop staring at her angelic face. For the uncountable stars were shining through her now.

The man was able to walk home.

After that there was always a line outside Suzama's house. She continued to perform many healings, although only a few matched her healing of the crippled man. For many seriously ill people she was unable to do anything. It is their karma to be ill, she would say. They had the word karma in that part of the world at that time, and they understood its meaning.

More than healing, Suzama preferred to foretell the future and to teach meditation. A series of special meditation techniques had come to her in visions and each of them was related to the worship of the Goddess Isis, the White Goddess, who shone in each soul above the head. Suzama taught mantra and breathing techniques, and sometimes she mixed the two together. I was her first student, as well as her last. While doing the practices she showed me, I began to experience peace of mind. She was my guru as well as my friend, and I always felt deeply indebted to her.

A time came when Suzama's exploits reached the ears of the rulers of the land. The king at that time was named Namok, and his queen was Delar. Namok was forty years older than his wife, and their beliefs, so the rumors said, were contrary to each other. Namok was firmly behind the powerful priest caste at the time, the fabled Setians, who supposedly gained divine insight from the ancient past, as well as from beings in the sky. The Setians worshipped a number of angry-looking deities, all of which were reptilian. I was curious, at the time, why Isis was supposed to be married to Osiris, who was Set's brother. The deities couldn't have been more different. The Setians did not approve of Isis worship, and went out of their way to destroy it. That is why Suzama always conducted her initiations in secret.

But the secret was out as far as Suzama's foretelling abilities were concerned. She was summoned to the Great Pyramid, and as her closest friend, I was allowed to come with her. In fact, Suzama refused to go without me. By this time she knew of my great physical power and felt safer with me by her side.

It seemed that Queen Delar had had a dream the Setian priests and priestesses were unable to decipher, at least to the queen's satisfaction. Delar wanted Suzama to try. Together, we were ushered into the royal meeting room. Its opulence was breathtaking. Never again would Egypt have such wealth, not even in the supposed golden ages of latter years. The very floor we walked on was made of gold.

Both king and queen were present, old and shrewd Namok on his high throne, with his tall and muscular spiritual adviser, Ory, at his right shoulder. Delar sat beside him on her own throne, with her young but hard face. It was Delar who bid us come closer and I couldn't help noticing out of the corner of my eye how Ory watched me. It was as if he had seen me before, or at least had had my features described to him. I wondered if his army of secret police, the dread Setian initiates, who had eyes like snakes, had taken note of my nocturnal ways. Ory wore a special dagger in his silver belt with which, it was reported, he cut out enemies' eyes before eating them. At that time the soul was thought to reside in the eyes.

Delar cleared her royal throat and spoke.

"You are Suzama. Your reputation precedes you. But who is this other person you have brought with you?"

Suzama bowed. "This is Sita, my queen. She is an Aryan—which is why her skin is fairer than ours. She is my friend and confidante. I ask your permission that she be allowed to remain by my side while I complete your reading."

Delar was curious about me. "Are you from India, Sita? I have heard stories of that land."

I also bowed. "Yes, my queen. I am far from home, yet I am happy to be a guest in your great land."

"What brought you to our land?" Ory asked. "Were you fleeing from danger?"

"No, my lord. It is only a love of adventure that brought me here."

Ory paused and whispered something in Namok's ear. The king frowned and nodded. But Ory smiled as he asked his next question and I couldn't help noticing how flat his eyes were. His hand never moved far from his dagger.

"It seems improper that a woman of your age should have traveled so far alone," he said. "Who were your companions along the road, Sita?"

"Merchants, my lord. They know the road to India well."

"Then you are also a merchant," Ory persisted.

"No," I said. "I have no special title."

"But you live in the house of slaves," Ory said. "Suzama is a slave. You, too, must be a slave."

I held his eye and there was strength in my gaze.

"No one owns me, my lord," I said.

My answer seemed to amuse Ory. He didn't reply but the power in my eyes did not seem to affect him. Perhaps he had goaded me on purpose, I thought.

Delar cleared her throat once more. "Come closer, Suzama and Sita. I will tell you my dream. If you are able to decipher it, your reward will be great."

Suzama bowed. "I will try my queen. But tell me first—did you have this dream at the last full moon?"

Delar was impressed. "I did indeed. How did you know?"

"I was not sure. But dreams that come at that time are particularly auspicious. Please tell me your dream, my queen."

"I was standing on a wide field in tall grass with lush rolling hills all around. It was night, but the sky was bright with more stars than we normally see on the clearest of nights. Many of these stars were deep blue. In the distance was a group of people who were walking into a ship that gave off a brilliant violet light. I was supposed to be on that ship, I knew, but before I could leave I had to talk to a beautifully dressed man. He stood nearby with a gold flute in his hand. He had bewitching dark eyes, was dressed in a blue robe, and had long dark hair. Around his neck was an exquisite jewel—it shone with many colored lights and hypnotized me. As I stared into it, he asked me, 'What is it you wish to know?' And I said, 'Tell me the law of life.' I don't know why I asked this question, but he said, 'This is the eternal law of life.' And he pointed his finger at me."

Delar paused. "That was the entire dream. It was incredibly vivid. When I woke from it I was filled with great wonder, but also great confusion. It seemed I was given a great secret but I don't understand what it is. Can you help me?"

"A moment please, my queen," Suzama said. Then she turned to me and spoke in whispers. "You have had dreams like this?"

My eyes widened. "Yes. How did you know?"

Suzama merely smiled. "Who is the man?"

"Lord Krishna. There is no doubt."

"And why did he point at her?"

"I don't know. Krishna often taught with riddles. He was mischievous."

"He was careful," Suzama said to me before turning back to the queen. "Delar, the answer to your dream is very simple."

Both the king and the queen sat up in anticipation. Even Priest Ory seemed to lean forward. He was no doubt one of those who had failed to decipher the dream properly.

"The blue stars signify the blue light of divinity," Suzama said. "You stood on a spiritual world in the spiritual sky. The man beside you was the Lord himself, come to give you instructions before you were born into this world. You asked the question you did because you wanted to know what law of life you should follow as queen of this land. You wanted to know what was fair, a means by which you could decide how to pass judgment on those you knew you would rule." Suzama paused. "He gave you the means when he pointed his finger at you."

Delar frowned. "I don't understand."

"Point your finger at me, my queen," Suzama said.

The queen did so. Suzama smiled.

"When you point your finger at someone, anyone, it is often a moment of judgment. We point our fingers when we want to scold someone, point out what they have done wrong. But each time we point, we simultaneously point three other fingers back at ourselves."

The queen looked down at her hand and gasped. "You are right. But what does that mean?"

"It means you must be very careful in your judgments," Suzama said. "Each time you decide fairly about someone, you gain three times the merit. But each time you make a poor judgment, you incur three times the debt. That is the law of life, whether you are a queen or a priest or a slave. When we do something good, it comes back to us threefold. When we harm someone, we harm ourselves three times as much." Suzama paused. "The Lord was telling you to be kind and good, my queen."

Queen Delar was impressed.

King Namok was unsure.

The high priest Ory was annoyed.

The main players in the drama were set.

The dice had been thrown.

It was only a question of how they would land.

And who would be left alive to collect the promised reward.

13 ～～

Back in Los Angeles the same day, I do not drive straight to my home in Pacific Palisades, but I do call to see if everyone is safe. Seymour says there is no sign of either the cops or Kalika. It sounds as if he has been enjoying Dr. Seter's company, but I don't think joy is a word I could attach to his relationship with James. I promise Seymour I will be home soon.

At five in the evening I am once more in the living room of Mrs. Hawkins, in the very house Eric longed to return to before his throat was cut open by my daughter. Hot-tempered Mr. Hawkins is fortunately not at home with Mrs. Hawkins. As before, she is plump and kindly, always fussing with her hands. Curiously, since I am associated with the kidnapping and death of her son, she does not appear unduly afraid of me. Indeed, she promptly invites me in when I come to the door. But perhaps she believed me the last time I visited, when I told her I did everything I could to save Eric.

"Would you like something to drink?" she asks as she takes a seat across from me.

"No, thank you." I pause. "You don't seem surprised to see me again."

Her face twitches with the painful memory of her dead son. Truly it is not the tragedies that destroy us, but the memories of them. Clearly not a minute goes by when she does not think about Eric.

"I thought I would see you again," she says.

"Why?"

"You just flew in that night, and then flew back out like a bird. My husband and I have talked about that a lot since you were here." She flashes a sad smile. "I think we convinced ourselves you weren't a devil, but an angel."

"I'm sorry I'm not an angel. I'm sorry I wasn't able to save your son."

She stops fussing with her hands for a moment. "You really tried, didn't you?"

"Yes." I lower my head. "I tried everything I knew."

She nods quietly. "That's what I told my husband. He didn't believe you at first, but maybe he does now." A pause. "Are you sure I can't get you something? I just baked some chocolate-chip cookies. Eric used to love them."

I look up and smile. "Sure. I would love a cookie."

She stands. "I have milk as well. You can't enjoy a cookie without milk."

"Ain't that the truth." I have to sit in the pain of the house while she busies herself in the kitchen. Since my rebirth I have noticed I sense the *feelings* of a place much more acutely. The chair where I sit feels as if it has been used to electrocute people. It is Mr. Hawkins's seat, I realize. He wanted to keep me from leaving the last time I came to visit. He wanted to call the cops.

Yet I also smell something as I wait for Mrs. Hawkins to return.

The foul odor of illness. A human would never detect it, but I do.

Mrs. Hawkins bustles in with a plate of cookies and a glass of milk.

"You must have more than one," she says, setting the plate before me. "Really, Eric and my husband used to finish a whole plate of these in a single afternoon. But with Eric gone and my— Well, Ted just doesn't seem as hungry as he used to be."

I pick up a cookie. "I'll have at least two."

She sits back down across from me. "You never told us your name last time, dear. Don't worry, I won't tell it to the police. I would just like to know what to call you."

"It's Alisa."

"Where are you from, Alisa?"

"Lots of places." I sip the milk. It is cold, good. The questions need to be asked but I find myself postponing them.

"I'm taking the year off from college, but I'll be in school next year. I just got accepted to SC. I'm going to major in pre-med."

"How do they taste?" she asks.

"Very good." But I end up putting the cookie down, half eaten. "Mrs. Hawkins, may I ask you a delicate question? It concerns Eric."

She hesitates. "What is the question?"

"Your son wanted to be a doctor. He said he wanted to follow in your husband's footsteps. Now I've met your husband, and he seemed like an intense and driven man. That is not a criticism but an observation. Eric was not so driven, yet I imagine some of that intensity must have rubbed off on him."

"That's true," she admits carefully.

"You see, this is hard for me. I don't want to walk on your pain, and I apologize if I am. But I was just wondering why, if Eric was so keen to be a doctor, he was taking a year off from college? I mean, I know a break from studying is not so unusual," I pause, "but was there a special reason for his extended vacation?"

She stares blankly for a moment. "Yes."

"May I know the reason?"

A tear runs down her cheek. "Eric had cancer. Lymphoma. It had spread through most of his body. It had gone into remission three times but it always came back." She swallows thickly. "The doctors said he had less than three months to live."

"I see." I am stunned. Eric had told me he wasn't well. Kalika had told me the same thing. Indeed, she had implied that was one of the reasons she killed him. So that he would have a better birth in his next life.

"I'm your daughter. You should believe me. I believe you even when I hear you lying to me."

Perhaps Kalika had told me the truth.

Mrs. Hawkins sobs quietly.

"There were a couple of police officers who came to the door the day Eric died," I say carefully. "They were looking for him, but the person I told you about—the one who killed your son—she convinced them to go off with her. And I never saw those men again. I assumed this woman killed them as well. But I never saw an article in the paper about them, and you know what big news any police killing is. I was just wondering, in your conversation with the police about your son, after his body was found, did they make any mention of the fact that they had lost two men?"

Mrs. Hawkins wipes at her face. "No."

I speak out loud, but mainly to myself. "It seems they would have, don't you think? If the disappearance was tied up with the same case as your son's death?"

"I would think so. Maybe the police are all right."

I pick up the cookie again, thinking.

"How did you get on with the policemen?"

"Fine."

"Are they fine?"

"You don't have to worry about them, Mother."

"They might be all right," I say.

Maybe I am worrying about all the wrong things.

14

The night I turned myself back into a vampire, I went searching for an ounce of Yaksha's blood to serve as an auroic catalyst. The only place to look, I thought, was the ice-cream truck where Eddie Fender had kept Yaksha's tortured body in cold storage. There I found the blood I needed, frozen beneath a box of Popsicles. But before I scraped it from the floor of the refrigerated compartment, I had a highly unusual conversation with an elderly homeless man with thinning white hair and a grimy face. He was obviously down on his luck. But when I strode up to say hello, he reacted as if he was expecting me.

"You look very nice tonight. But I know you're in a hurry."

"How do you know I'm in a hurry?"

"I know a few things. You want this truck I suppose. I've been guarding it for you."

"How long have you been here?"

"I don't rightly know. I think I've been here since you were last here."

The ice-cream truck should not have been there. The police should have hauled it away a couple of months earlier. Yet not only was the truck parked where it had been when it held Yaksha, the refrigerator unit was still working, and the homeless man implied he had kept it working for me. That was crucial, because if the blood had melted and rotted, it would have been of no use to me. I wouldn't have been able to turn back into a vampire. I would have possessed no special abilities with which to protect the child.

Now the big question was . . .

Did the homeless man know that?

He obviously knew something.

The bigger question was *how* he knew.

With the sun setting and with no better place to go, I return to the street where I met the man. There, to my utter astonishment, I find him sitting near the spot where the ice-cream truck had been parked. It is gone but the man has not changed. In fact, he is drinking a carton of milk as he was the last time we met. He looks up as I approach and his eyes sparkle in the dull yellow light of the street lamps. He doesn't rise, though. He is an old man and getting up is hard on his knees. I remember I had to help him up the last time. He flashes me a warm smile.

"Why if it isn't you again," he says. "I thought you might come back."

"Have you been waiting for me?" I ask.

"Sure. I don't mind waiting around. Don't have a lot to do these days, you know."

I crouch by his side. "What do you do when you're not waiting for me?"

He is shy. "Oh, I just move around, pick up an odd job here and there, help out where I can."

I smile. "Well, you sure helped me last time."

He is pleased. "That's good. But you're a bright girl. You know how to help yourself." He stops. "Hey, would you like to play a game of cards?"

I raise an eyebrow. "Poker?"

He brushes his hand. "No. That's too hard a game for an old fella like me. You have to think too much. How about a game of twenty-one? I'll be the house. I'll play by house rules. I'll hit on every sixteen and give you a tip every now and then if you need it. As long as you promise to tip me if you win in the end. How does that sound? You know how to play twenty-one?"

I sit cross-legged in front of him. "I am a born gambler. Do you have cards?"

He reaches in his old coat pocket and pulls out a pack. "Do I have cards? These are fresh from a high roller's blackjack table in Las Vegas. Mind if I shuffle? Those are house rules, you know. Dealer has to shuffle."

"You shuffle. What are we betting?"

He takes a sip of his milk as he opens the pack. "It doesn't matter." Then he laughs and the sound is like music to my ears because it has been so long since I have heard the sound of pure joy. "An old bum like me—I have nothing to lose!"

I laugh with him. "What's your name, old bum?"

He pauses and catches my eye. "Now just one moment. You're the youngster here. You've never told me your name."

I offer my hand. "I'm Sita."

He shakes my hand. "Mike."

"Where are you from, Mike?"

He lets go of my hand and shuffles the cards. He is a pro with them; he obviously can shuffle both sides of the deck with as few as five fingers. Yet a trace of sorrow enters his voice. The tone is not painful, more bittersweet.

"Lots of places, Sita," he says. "You know how it is when you get as old as I am, one place blurs into another. But I try to keep moving, try to keep my hand in. Where are you from?"

"India."

He is impressed. "By golly, that's far away! You must have had plenty of adventures between here and India."

"Too many adventures, Mike. But are you going to stop talking and start dealing? I'm getting anxious to beat you at what I know is your favorite game."

He acts offended, although he is still smiling.

"Hold on just one second," he says. "We haven't decided what we're wagering. What have you got?"

"Money."

He nods. "Money is good. How much you got?"

I reach in my back pocket. "Three hundred dollars in cash."

He whistles. "My sweet lord! You carry your bankroll on you. Now I know that ain't smart, no sir."

I flip open my wad of twenties. Got them from an ATM machine down the street.

"I don't mind betting this. What are you betting?"

My question seems to catch him off guard. He asks with a trace of suspicion, "What do you want?"

"Oh. Just a few friendly hints, what you offered. Can you give me some of those? When I win I mean?"

He speaks with mock confidentiality. "You don't need them when you win, girl. You need them when you lose." He begins to deal the cards. "Sure, I'll help you out. Just don't you get too rough on old Mike."

I throw a twenty down. "I'll try to behave myself."

He deals me a fifteen, bust hand. He is looking strong, showing a ten. He peeks at his hole card and grins. By the rules, I know I should hit. But I hate chasing a strong hand with so little room to maneuver. He waits for me to make a decision, a sly grin on his old lips.

"Going to risk it?" he asks, teasing me.

"Sure." I scratch the ground between us. "Hit me."

I get a seven. Twenty-two. Bust. I'm twenty down.

He deals another hand. I get eleven, and he shows a six, the weakest card he can show. By most house rules I am allowed to double down at this point. But I ask if it is OK to be sure. He nods, pleased to hit me again. I don't know what he'll do if he gets in my debt. I lay another twenty beside my turned-over cards and he deals me a card.

"A nine," I mutter. "Twenty. I'm sitting pretty."

"You are pretty, Sita," he says as he flips over his cards, showing a five, a total of eleven. He draws and gets a ten, twenty-one, beating me by one again. My forty belongs to him.

"Damn," I mutter.

I lose the next six hands. Every decision I make is wrong, yet I am playing by the book. The published rules say I should win about half the hands. Yet I don't think he is cheating me, even though he seems to take great pleasure in taking my money. He already has two hundred bucks, two-thirds of my bankroll. If I don't win soon I'll have to walk.

On the ninth hand he deals me a natural. Blackjack.

He is showing only a seven. I have finally won.

He offers me a twenty. The amount I bet.

"You want it?" he asks, and there is a gleam in his eye.

"You were going to give me a tip," I say.

"But you won. Fate favored you, Sita, you didn't have to do anything. When a winning hand is coming around, it's going to come no matter what." He gathers the cards together. He is down to the bottom of the deck; he has to shuffle again. He comments on the fact, as an aside. "You know if this was a casino and I had myself a shoe, I could deal as many as six decks without shuffling. What do you think of that?"

I go completely numb.

But it will be dark angels that force him and his mother to flee to the mirror in the sky, where shoes move without feet and the emerald circle is seen in the morning light.

Lake Tahoe, I remember suddenly, was called "the mirror in the sky" by the original Indians who lived in the area, because they had to hike up the mountain to reach it, and then, it was such a large, clear lake, it looked to them like a perfect mirror reflecting the sky. Also, there is a small but gorgeous cove in the lake called Emerald Bay. Finally, there are casinos nearby that have special shoes for playing twenty-one. As we are playing twenty-one right now, only without one of those shoes that moves without feet.

Kalika had a book on Lake Tahoe.

Mike stares at me. "Want to play another hand?"

I slowly shake my head. "It's not necessary, thank you."

He nods as he reads my expression. "I guess you'll be on your way now. I'm sorry to see you go."

I gaze into his bright eyes. "Are you sorry, Mike?"

He shrugs. "I know you have a job to do. I don't

want to interfere with that none. It's just that I like it when you stop by, you know. It reminds me of when I was young."

"I'm older than I look. You must know that."

He gives me a wistful expression. "Well, I suppose I do. But I have to say you're still a youngster to me."

I lean forward and hug him, and feel his bony ribs, his dirty clothes, and his love. A powerful feeling sweeps over me, as if I have finally found a member of a family I never knew existed. But the hug can last only so long. He is right—I have a job to do. Letting go, I climb to my feet. The thought of leaving him is painful. I have to ask the next question even though I know he will not give me a straight answer.

"Will you be here when I return?"

He scratches his head and takes a sip from his milk carton. For a moment he appears slightly bewildered. He quickly counts the money he has won and stuffs it in his coat pocket. Then he coughs and looks up and down and street to see if anyone is listening. Finally he looks at me again.

"I'm sorry, Sita, I don't rightly know. I'm always moving around, like I said, trying to keep my hand in. But I hope I see you again." He pauses. "I like your spirit."

I lean over and kiss his forehead.

"I like your spirit, Mike. Be here for me again. Please?"

He flashes a faint smile. "I'll see what I can do."

15 ~~~

The inevitable happened. Queen Delar became a student of Suzama's and a short time after the dream reading, Suzama privately initiated the queen in a small room in Suzama's own home. Suzama refused to do it in the Great Pyramid, saying the vibrations in there would never recover from Ory and the evil Setian initiations. Also, Suzama did not want the powerful priests to know what was happening. She asked the queen to keep quiet about her practices for the time being. Suzama knew King Namok did not have long to live.

Six months later the king did die, and Queen Delar moved more boldly than Suzama wished.

The queen immediately proclaimed her spiritual path via the Isis techniques and encouraged any who wished to follow Suzama to do so. Yet the queen was wise enough not to make it a state order. Suzama refused to teach anyone who was forced into the practice. At the same time the queen instructed a large team of laborers to build a temple to Isis not far from the Great Pyramid, which Suzama refused to enter. The queen wanted an elaborate temple but Suzama persuaded her to construct a modest building, and so Suzama had her own place in which to teach within a year of the king's death. Suzama filled it with plants and flowers and different-colored crystals brought from all over the continent.

Naturally, during this period, the Setians suffered a great setback as far as their influence was concerned. Yet the queen did not banish them from the land, because Suzama had advised her not to. I questioned my friend about not banishing them. But Suzama felt so strongly about freedom of thought that she even protected what was clearly an evil group. Yet I doubt if even Suzama knew how many assassins Ory sent to dispose of Suzama and me. Of course, none of those assassins ever returned to their leader, even when they came in groups of three and four. I seldom rested in those days and never sat with my back to a door.

But I never drank Setian blood. Just the smell of it filled me with bad feelings. The group was definitely working with subtle powers of some kind, and I began to pay more heed to their rumored contacts with an ancient reptilian race, which they achieved through a mind-meld process that used identical twins as catalysts. Even more important, I began to investigate their rumored liaisons with the direct remains of the same race, which now existed on different worlds circling other suns. I knew the Setians were getting their power from somewhere else, and I wanted to find the root of it. Yet I made little progress.

Even the Setians I killed had great strength in their eyes, a magnetic field they could generate to subdue weaker wills. Naturally, their power did not work on me, but I could see the effect on the people in the city, wherever they were allowed to speak. Suzama should have been welcomed as a great prophet and the masses should have embraced her teachings, yet her following, even when her temple was complete, was relatively small. The Setians were constantly stirring up hate and lies against her.

Fortunately, Suzama did shield the queen from Ory and his cult. Queen Delar wouldn't even meet with Ory once the king died, although I did see Ory from time to time. Even though he was always polite to me, I never failed to hear the hiss of a snake beneath his breath. Why shouldn't I recognize it? In a sense we were cousins. Yaksha, a yashini by nature, had created me. And the yashinis were well known in India as a race of mystical serpents.

Yet Ory never reminded me of Yaksha, who loved Krishna above all things. And my power to influence the wills of others was much different from the power of the Setians. For their power left their victims weak and disoriented. Many never recovered from it and this power became known by the seldom spoken name of *seedling,* because it sowed seeds of consciousness that were not one's own.

I could see that matters would eventually come to a head with the Setians, only the climax came more quickly and with a destructive force greater than I could ever have imagined. Suzama was only nineteen when I received a personal invitation from Ory. He wanted to meet me alone in the desert so that we could discuss our differences and try to put an end to our conflict. This was only six days after I had slain ten of his people who had stolen into the Temple of Isis in the middle of the night. Ory had never sent so many before and I had been lucky to kill them all. Had he sent twice the number both Suzama and I would have died. Actually, I wondered why he had not, which should have served as a warning to me.

I sent back a messenger saying I would be happy to meet him.

He planned to kill me as surely as I planned to kill him.

Before heading to the desert I met with Suzama to tell her my plans. She was in her inner chamber in the temple and in a particularly reflective mood. She was writing when I entered but put aside the papyrus so that I could not see it. Her usual warm greeting was missing. Before I could speak, she wanted to know why I was dressed for the desert.

"You are wrong to think your enemies possess any virtues," I say. "I tire of our always having to be on guard. I am meeting with Ory tonight deep in the desert. He has chosen the spot but I know it well. When the head vanishes, the body falls. It will end tonight."

But Suzama shook her head. "This is not my will. You have not asked my permission. Tonight the stars are particularly inauspicious. Cancel the meeting right now."

I sat beside her. She almost seemed to disappear in the large silk cushions. Dressed in a simple white robe, she wore a blue scarf around her neck. Woven inside it were threads of gold that outlined all the constellations in the sky, even those seen from the bottom of the world. The latter, Suzama said, she had seen in visions. I had no doubt they were correct, even though I would not listen to her when it came to Ory. It was my turn to shake my head.

"I never told you how many of his people I slew last week," I said.

"How many?"

"Ten."

She grimaced. "In here?"

"I was able to deal with most of them outside. But there will be more if I don't destroy Ory now."

"But you don't know Ory. You don't know what he is."

"Of course I do. He is a Setian."

Suzama spoke gravely. "He is a real Setian. Just as you are no longer human, he is not one of our kind. Those he sent to kill us before were mere students." She paused. "I suspect he is not from this world."

"I don't care," I say. "If he comes alone, I can

deal with him. And if he doesn't, then I will know and decide what to do. But I know I must face him. It is foolish to wait."

Suzama was reflective. "Wisdom is not always logical."

"Lacking your wisdom, I can only decide based on what I see and know."

She stroked my leg, which was bare beneath my robe.

"You know, I foresaw this conversation," she said. "Nothing I say to you right now will change your mind. That is because of who you are and because of the stars above. They pretend to be your stars but they're not." She paused and spoke as if she were far away. "They are arranged as they were the night you were transformed into a vampire."

I am shocked. "Is this true?"

She nods solemnly. "The serpent walked the forest. The lizard crawls in the sand. It is the same difference." She squeezed my leg and her eyes were damp. "Tonight is a time of transformation for you. Do you understand what I'm saying?"

"Yes. Death is the biggest transformation. Ory might kill me."

"Yes. It is possible."

"You don't know for sure?"

She was a long time answering.

"No. The Divine Mother does not show me." She shook herself and came back to Earth, for a moment. She kissed the side of my face. "Words are useless tonight, even written words. Go then, and go with light. I will wait here for you. I will be here when you return."

I hug her. "I owe you a great deal. Tonight, perhaps I can repay you."

There was a place twenty miles from the city, deep in the desert, called the Bowl of Flies. In the late spring the flies would be so thick there during the day that it would be hard to breathe without inhaling them. Yet at night they would all but vanish, and there was no reason to explain why they came at all. There was nothing for the flies to eat, unless a small animal chanced to die there. But then again, an unusual number of animals did collapse in that spot. Even a bird could seize up in midflight and fall dead into the place.

Ory wanted to meet me in the bowl.

I arrived early to see if he had assassins hidden. The area appeared empty for far around. There was no moon but I didn't need it. My eyes were not drawn to the sky as they usually were when the stars were so bright. Suzama's words continued to haunt me. She had ended our good-bye almost in midsentence. *Words are useless now.*

Ory was suddenly there, sitting on a camel.

It was strange how I hadn't heard him approach.

He got down off his animal and slowly moved toward me. I had also come on a camel but had sent my beast off. For me to run twenty miles across the desert at night was nothing. On the way home I hoped to be carrying Ory's head. Like me, he wore a long naked sword in his belt, along with his sharp dagger. Listening closely, I could still detect no others, and I thought him a fool to meet me under such circumstances. Yet he smiled as he approached, his huge bald head shiny even in the faint starlight. It smelled as if he had oiled his skull before coming, a disgusting ointment smell.

"Sita," he said. "I thought maybe you would not come."

I mocked him. "It is not often I am granted an exclusive audience with such a renowned spiritual figure."

"Do you know whence our spiritual power comes?"

"An unhappy place. A place without love or compassion. I do not know the name of this place, but I do know I never want to go there."

He stood close, yet his hands stayed clear of his sword. He gestured to the sky. "This world is not the only one. There are many kingdoms for us to rule, and I can gain you safe passage to these other places, if you will join me. I have watched you closely these last two years, Sita, and I know you are one of us. You have power, you take what you wish. You kill as a matter of course to satisfy your hunger, to satisfy your lust for life. You move without the burden of conscience. Yet you hide behind the dress of that slave fortune teller. This I do not understand."

"I hide behind no one. Suzama is much more than a seer of the future. She sees into the hearts of men and women. She brings peace where there is pain, healing where there is sickness. The Setians do none of these things. They are interested in power for power's sake. Nothing could be more boring to me, or more offensive. You think we are kin only because I am strong. But that is the only thing we have in common, and before this night is over, even that will not be true. Because you will be buried in the sand, and I will be laughing in the city as I free it of the last of your kind."

He was amused at that. "Does your blessed Suzama permit such killings?"

"I will tell Suzama about it after I am done."

"And you think you could destroy all Setians so easily?"

I shrugged. "I have had no trouble in the past."

He came close and his smile vanished. "You are a fool. I sent mere apprentices to test your strength. In all the time you have been in the city, you have met fewer than a handful of our secret order. And you didn't even know them when you met them. We seldom come out from the depths of the Great Pyramid. Only I, Ory, the leader regularly attends to the things of this world. But I will not share this world with another, neither you nor Suzama. It is your choice. You join us now, and swear a sacred oath to me, or you will not leave this place alive."

I laughed. "You keep telling me what I don't know. I tell you that you don't know what I am." I drew my sword. "The blood that runs in my veins is not human, but I have the strength of many humans. Draw your sword and fight me, Ory. Die like a soldier rather than a coward and fake priest who puts silly spells on unsuspecting souls."

But he did not draw his sword. He lifted his arms upward.

A strange red light shimmered in his eyes.

His voice, as he spoke, boomed like thunder.

"Behold the night of Set, the will of those who

came before humanity. It lives inside the stars that shine with the light of blood. Look up and see what force you think to defy."

Such was the strength in his voice, that I did glance up for a moment. To my utter astonishment the night sky had changed. Above me were fresh constellations laid over the old ones. They shone with brilliant red stars that seemed to pulse like stellar hearts feeding the burning blood of one huge ravenous cosmic being. Just the sight of them filled me with nausea. How had he managed to change the heavens? He must be a powerful sorcerer, I thought.

I drew my sword and moved toward him to cut off his head.

But there was flash of green light.

The metal of my sword flowed like liquid onto the sand.

My hand burned, the flesh literally black. The pain was so excruciating that I was forced to my knees. Ory towered over me, and behind his large skull the red stars seemed to grow even brighter. It was as if a bunch of them had clustered together and begun to move toward us. Through the mist of my agony I saw them form a circle and begin to spin. The very air seemed to catch fire around them. Ory gloated over me.

"We Setians control the elements," he said. "That was fire, in case you didn't know. Now I will show you the earth element."

He laid his big foot on my chest and kicked hard. He was many times stronger than I, I realized too late. Crashing down hard on my back, my arms spread out to my sides as if I were about to be crucified. No doubt that was the effect he was searching for. Before I could bring them back up and defend myself, the red stars over his head seemed to throb again and I heard the sand crack on both sides. For a moment it seemed alive, the very ground, liquid mud shot through with veins of brains, and I watched in horror as it reached out like a thick fist and grabbed my lower arms and covered my hands. Then the sand turned to stone and I could not move. All this seemed to happen in a moment. Ory withdrew his dagger and knelt beside me and held the tip close to my eyes.

"Now you have seen a demonstration of real power," he said.

I spat in his face. "I am not impressed."

He wiped away the spit and played the tip of the dagger over my eyelids. "You are beautiful, Sita. You could have been mine. But I see now it would have been impossible to dominate you. Above all else a Setian must control those who are beneath him."

"Kill me and be done with it. I am tired of talking to you."

He smiled softly. "You will not die easily. I know how quickly your wounds can heal, but I also know that a deep wound cannot heal around a dagger such as this, which is poisoned, and which will fit nicely somewhere in your barren womb."

He stabbed me then, low down in my abdomen, and the blade burned like ice frozen from the tears of a thousand previous victims. I knew then that the stories about him and his dagger were true. He had cut out many eyes and eaten them in front of his victims. But he wouldn't blind me now because he wanted me to see the sun when it rose, and the millions of flies that would cover my body. His poison was subtle, not designed to immediately kill, but to draw out my agony.

I noticed that the red stars were no longer in the sky.

Ory stood and climbed back onto his camel.

"The earth can move as easily in the city as it can in this place," he said. "When the sun is high in the sky, the Temple of Isis will be buried along with your precious Suzama. You may hear the destruction even from here. Just know that the flies that feed here are always hungry, and that it will not be long before you join her."

"Ory!" I called as he rode off.

He paused. "Yes Sita?"

"I will see you again someday. It is not over."

"For you it is." He laughed as he rode away.

The sun rose and the flies came. Slowly my wound bled and steadily my pain increased. It seemed as if the desert wind were fire and the sky rained darts. The sound of the many flies sucking on my blood was enough to drive me mad. The filthy insects polluted my soul as much as my wound. All I had to look forward to was the midday sun, when my friend would die. I had a feeling I would hear something.

The day wore on. Breathing became a nightmare. Existence itself was the greatest torture. How I prayed to die then, for the first time ever. How I cursed Krishna. Where was his fabled grace now? I had not disobeyed him. Only he had set me up before an unstoppable foe. There was no hope for the world, I realized. The Setians were worse than a million vampires. And they were spreading across the stars.

The sun reached its high point. It was a red sun.

The interior of my skull began to boil and I heard myself scream.

Then the noise came, waves of rolling thunder. The ground began to shake, then to dance, tearing apart at the seams. The frozen sand that bound my arms and legs cracked, and I would have been able to stand if the entire desert had not suddenly been transformed into a torrential ocean. What had Ory set in motion? The elements had gone insane. The earth believed it was water. Beyond the Bowl of Flies I heard sand dunes pitch and break like waves upon a shore.

Then it stopped and all was silent.

Pulling out the dagger, I brushed off the flies and crawled out of the bowl. When I reached the upper rim, I stared at a desert I did not recognize.

It was entirely flat.

Slowly, for me, my wound healed.

Somehow I managed to stagger back to the city. Ory's poison was still in my veins but maybe it had lost some of its potency. When the city finally came into view, I saw that Ory's day had passed, as had Suzama's. Either Ory had lost control of his precious earth element or else Suzama had seized control of it at the last moment and stuffed it down his throat. The worship of Isis and Set was over for that time.

A gash in the earth as thick as the Great Pyramid had opened up and swallowed the bulk of the city. The pyramid and all the other temples were gone. Those buildings that had not fallen into the chasm were nevertheless flattened. A handful of survivors stumbled around in the midst of this destruction but few looked as if they still possessed their wits.

I searched for Suzama but never found her.

Not long afterward I left Egypt.

16 ~~~

We cannot get a flight to Lake Tahoe or even into Reno. San Francisco is our next best choice. The four of us, Seymour, James, Dr. Seter, and I, fly to San Francisco and rent a car in the Bay Area. Airport security has not allowed us to take weapons with us, so along the way, close to ten o'clock, I have the others wait while I break into a gun shop and steal two shotguns and several rounds of ammunition. James seems impressed when I get back to the car. He sits up front with me while Seymour talks to Dr. Seter in the backseat. The doctor is not looking good, and I wonder if he suffered a mild heart attack the previous night.

"How did you get into the store?" James asks as

we race back onto the freeway and head east at high speed.

"I picked the lock," I say, doing the driving.

"Did an alarm go off?" James asks.

"Not one that I could hear." I glance over my shoulder. "Do you need to use the restroom, Dr. Seter? There's a gas station a couple of miles ahead."

His face is ghastly white but he shakes his head. "We don't have time. We have to get there before she does." He pauses. "I'm still furious at myself that I didn't allow you to see all of the scripture the first night. How were you able to decipher the clues as to the child's location so quickly?"

"I had a little help," I say.

"From whom?" James asks.

"You wouldn't believe me if I told you."

"I think everyone in this car is ready to believe anything," Seymour mutters.

"Ain't that the truth," Dr. Seter says.

Yet I hesitate to talk about Mike. "A little bird helped me."

James gently persists. "Does this bird have a name?"

I give him a look. "Not that I can remember."

We reach the mountains surrounding Lake Tahoe and I plow up the winding road that leads to the lake. The others sit, clutching the ceiling grips; I have rented a Lexus sports coupe and I push the car to its limit. Dr. Seter looks as if he will vomit over the backseat but he doesn't complain. There's too much at stake.

As we come over the rim of the mountain and see the lake, I smell Kalika. I am surprised at my own surprise because I should have expected her to be here, but in reality I didn't. Yet I still don't think she has deciphered Suzama's code before me. On the contrary, I think she is following us, using some invisible psychic tracking. I believe she still waits to see what moves we'll make next. And this is a paradox for me because I realize I might endanger the child most by trying to find it to protect it. Certainly there must have been a reason why my daughter has left so many of us alive. She didn't know where I was when I was at the hospital with the child. Yet she knew where I was when I was living in Pacific Palisades with Seymour. I have to wonder if the child has a mystical shield around him that Kalika can't pierce but maybe I can.

It may not matter.

If I can smell her, she can see us.

But I cannot have come this far just to turn away from the child. I cannot trust in my theories. I only know that if I can find Paula and her baby I can take them to some safe place. That is logical; it is something I can envision without employing the wisdom or intuition of Suzama. Starting downhill, I floor the accelerator and turn toward Emerald Bay.

We reach it twenty minutes later.

The spot is one of the most enchanting in all of nature. The bay is maybe two hundred yards across, sheltered on three sides by majestic cliffs with tall pines hugging them. The isthmus is narrow, giving the bay excellent shelter from the lake itself, which can get rough in stormy weather. There is a tiny island in the center of the water, a place for children to play and adults to relax. Even at midnight, beneath the brilliant moon, the circular bay is magical. But tonight it is silver, not emerald. Silver like the dagger Ory stabbed in me.

For some reason, I have to remind myself that that was long ago.

My abdomen cramps and I brush away a fly that has entered the car.

The odor of Kalika overpowers my other senses. Truly, since being touched by Yaksha's blood, my sense of smell has become my most potent weapon. Rolling down my window all the way, I use my nose like a needle on a compass, and it doesn't fail me. It points in only one direction, toward a small wooden house set on redwood stilts above an abandoned stone church at the floor of the cliff, not far above the water. The place is almost hidden in the trees, but I see it.

I drive faster.

I stop some distance from the house. The road we're on circles all of Lake Tahoe but at this place it is three hundred yards up the side of the mountain. Grabbing a shotgun and ignoring the others, I slip six shells into it. The remainder of the ammunition is in the box that I stuff into my pocket. Popping open the driver's door, I am almost outside when James grabs my arm.

"Where are you going?" he demands.

"Some things you can't help me with," I say.

"Alisa," Seymour says. The others only know me by that name.

"It has to be this way." I shake off James. "Stay and take care of one another. She may come this way yet."

I don't give them a chance to respond. Jumping out of the car, I run around the bend, and the moment I am out of sight I switch into hypermode. The tangled trees and uneven boulders don't even slow me. I reach the house in thirty seconds.

The front door has already been kicked in.

Kalika was watching which way my nose turned.

Inside I find Paula staring out a window that overlooks Emerald Bay. There is a small boat on the cold water, with an outboard motor softly churning through the night, heading away from us. Grabbing Paula from behind, I turn her around.

"Did she take the child?" I demand.

Pretty dark-haired Paula is the color of dirty snow.

"Yes," she says with a dry voice.

"Stay here." I pump my shotgun. "I will get him back."

The next moment finds me outside, running along the edge of the bay. In places this is difficult because the sides are sheer stone. When I come to such a spot I jump higher for any inch of ledge that will support my feet and keep running. Kalika's outboard motor is not very strong. I reach the isthmus seconds before her boat does. Dressed in a long white coat, the baby wrapped in a white blanket on her knees, she looks up at me as I raise my shotgun and take aim at her bow. She is only fifty yards away. Her eyes shimmer with the glow of the moon and she doesn't seem to be surprised.

The baby talks softly to her, infant nonsense. He is not afraid, but fear is almost all I know as I sight along the barrel and squeeze the trigger.

The blast of the shotgun echoes across the bay.

I have blown a hole in the front of the boat.

Water gushes in. Kalika grabs the handle of the outboard and turns the boat around. For a moment her back is to me, an easy shot. Yet I don't take it. I tell myself there is a chance I might hit the child. At first Kalika seems to be headed back toward the beach below Paula's house, but then it is clear the miniature island in the center of the bay is her goal. Perhaps the water is gushing in too fast. Kalika picks up the child and hugs him to her chest even before the boat reaches the island. Then she is up and out of the sinking craft, scampering up the dirt path that leads to a small abandoned house at the top of the island. Sliding the shotgun under my black leather coat, I dive off the low cliff and into the water.

The lake temperature is bracing, even for me. But vampires never like the cold, although we can tolerate it far better than human beings can. My stroke is hampered by my clothes and gun, but I reach the island in less than a minute. Shivering on the beach in the rays of the moon, I remove the shotgun and pump another round into the chamber. There is a good chance it will still fire. If it doesn't then this will be the last moonlit night of my life.

I find Kalika sitting on a bench in the stone house at the top of the island. It is not properly a house, more an open collection of old walls. Last time I was here a guide told me people came here for tea during the Second World War. Kalika sits with the baby on her lap, playing with him, oblivious of me and my shotgun. I feel I have to say something. Of course I am not fooled. I keep my weapon held ready.

Yet maybe I am the biggest fool of all.

"It is over," I say. "Set the child down."

Kalika doesn't even look up. "The floor is cold. He might catch cold."

I shake my gun. "I am serious."

"That is your problem."

"Kalika—"

"Do you know what name Paula gave the child?" she interrupts.

"No. I didn't stop to ask her."

"I think she named him John. That's what I've been calling him." Finally she looks at me. "But you know Mike, don't you?"

I am bewildered. "Yes. Have you spoken to him?"

"No. But I know him. He's a bum." She lifts the child to her breast. Kalika has a voluptuous figure; she could probably bear many healthy children. God knows what they would be like. She strokes the baby's soft skull. "I think we have company."

"What are you talking about?"

"Your friend is coming."

"Good," I say, although I don't hear anyone approaching. "More reason for you to surrender the child." I grow impatient. "Put him down!"

"No."

"I will shoot."

"No, you won't."

"You murdered two dozen innocent people. You ripped their hearts and heads off right in front of my eyes and you think I can still care for you? Well, you're wrong." I step closer and aim the shotgun at her face. "You are not immortal. If I fire and your brains splatter the wall behind you, then you will die."

She stares at me. We are out of the moonlight. There should be no light in her dark eyes at all. Nevertheless they shine with a peculiar white glow. I had thought it was red the last time I saw them during our confrontation on the pier. But maybe the color is not hers but mine. Maybe she is just a mirror for me, Kali Ma, the eternal abyss, who destroys time itself. My mother myself. I cannot look at her with the child and not think of when she was a baby.

"The body takes birth and dies," she says. "The eternal self is unmoved."

I shake my shotgun angrily. "You will move for me, goddamn you!"

Kalika smiles. She wants to say something.

But suddenly there is a blade at my throat.

"I will take that shotgun," James says softly in my ear.

I am surprised but not terribly alarmed.

"James," I say patiently, "I am not going to shoot the child."

He presses the blade tighter and forces my head back.

"I know that, Sita," he says calmly. "I still want the gun."

I swallow. Now I am concerned.

"How do you know my name?" I ask.

He grips the shotgun and carefully lifts it from my hands.

"We have met before," he says. "You just don't remember me."

"She remembers," Kalika says, standing now, her expression unfathomable.

James points the shotgun at her while he keeps the blade at my throat. Out of the corner of my eye I get a glimpse of it. A dagger of some kind, ancient design, cold metal. James is calm and cool. He gestures with the tip of the shotgun.

"You will set the child down on the bench beside you," he says to my daughter. "If you don't I will shoot, and you know I won't miss. Either of you."

Kalika does not react.

James scrapes me lightly with the knife and my throat bleeds.

"I will kill your mother," he says. "You will have to watch her die."

A shadow crosses Kalika's face. "No," she says.

James smiles. "You know me. You know I do not bluff."

Kalika nods slightly. Really, it is as if she knows him well.

"All right," she says in a soft, perhaps beaten, voice.

"Do it!" James orders.

Kalika turns to set the child down. The baby is almost out of her hands when I see her change her mind. Maybe James sees the same thing, I don't know. But he is ready for her when she suddenly grabs the baby and bolts. Kalika moves extraordinarily fast but James is no slouch when it comes to reflexes.

He shoots her in the lower back.

Kalika staggers but manages to hold on to the child. Keeping his blade tight to my throat, he pumps the shotgun again and takes aim. It is then I ram an elbow into his side. He seems ready for that as well, because even though I have hurt him, he manages to draw the blade all the way across my throat. And he doesn't just nick me. Suddenly my life's blood is pouring over my chest and James has got Kalika in his sights again and there is absolutely nothing I can do to stop him.

James shoots Kalika in the back, behind the heart.

Kalika is covered in blood. She tries to turn, perhaps to attack, but seeing James pumping again, she puts her back to him once more. He fires a third time, hitting her right shoulder. Kalika slumps to the floor, her right arm useless now. Still she manages to hold on to the child, to shelter him from the blasts that ravage her body. As I collapse to the floor, James pumps again and points the shotgun at Kalika's head, actually touching her left temple with the black barrel. He still has the dagger in his right hand and I finally recognize it.

Ory's knife. I feel his poison once more in my system.

I even recognize Ory's voice when James speaks next.

Funny how I didn't before. Too bad, huh.

"I just want the child," James says to my daughter.

She stares up at him. "Your kind never wants just one thing."

He pulls the trigger back dangerously far.

"You missed me at the condo," he says. "That was your chance. But you will have no more chances if you do not do what I say. Nor will the child."

Kalika stares up at him a moment.

Then she hands him the baby with her left arm.

He takes the infant in his knife arm.

He turns to walk away.

Kalika tries to get up.

"No!" I gasp, choking on my own blood.

James pivots and shoots her directly in the heart. Stunned, she staggers back. He pumps again and shoots her in the exact same spot. Her chest cavity literally explodes. Her white coat and white dress are a mess of red tissue and torn threads. Reaching out a feeble left arm, trying to give it one last desperate try, she suddenly closes her eyes and falls face first on the floor. James stares down at her for a moment and then drops the shotgun and kneels beside me. The infant's face is only inches from my own but I am unable to reach out and touch him. The baby seems worried, but James looks as if he is having a good time.

"What did you tell me?" he asks. "'I will see you again someday. It is not over.'" He pauses. "Yeah, I think that was it. Well, at least you were half right."

I drown in red blood. My voice bubbles out.

"How?"

"How am I here again in a different body? That is a Setian secret, isn't it? But to tell you the truth I never left. Oh, I have transferred many times, into many forms, but that is a small trick for beings such as ourselves." He glances at motionless Kalika. "It is a pity your daughter had to destroy my entire crop of new apprentices. But there will be more from where they came."

"What?" I whisper.

He chuckles. "What am I going to do with the child now that you have led me to him? Honestly, you don't want to know. Better you go to your grave with no horrific image in your pretty head." He raises the dagger. "Where do you want me to put in the poison? It is a new and improved brand. It is guaranteed to kill even the strongest of vampires. And slowly."

"Go to hell," I gasp.

"Sita, I just came from there."

He stabs me in midback and leaves the blade in. I am too weak to pull it out. To find it, even. James stands and walks away with the child.

Finally, I hear the infant begin to cry.

17 ~

Red, searing pain and black despair. These two colors, these two forms of torture, are all I know for the next few minutes. It is not as if I lose sight of the room, it is just that I see it from another angle. A place of pain and judgment where my soul floats above the boiling cauldron I am sure is waiting for me on the other side. To realize I have been working all along for the enemy, that I was in fact their greatest ally, is too much for me. Death, if it would just involve oblivion, would be more than welcome. But I know there must be a special hell prepared for the one who sold the messiah to the jackal.

From far away I feel something moist and warm touch my lips.

It tastes like blood, very sweet blood, but it is such a potent elixir that I swear I have never encountered it before. Before my mind knows it, my body is hungrily licking the substance. The flow of blood that has been steadily dripping from my throat finally begins to slow. At first I think it is because my body is running out of blood, but then I realize I am healing, which should be impossible with a severed neck, a knife in my back, and Setian poison pumping in my veins. Yet after a time my vision clears and I am able to see normally.

My daughter lies beside me.

She is feeding me her own blood with her cupped palm.

For a moment I think that means she is recovering. But then I see that her horrible wounds have not healed at all. My eyes register my sorrow but she smiles even now.

"There is only enough life left for you," she says.

I push her hand away. "You mustn't. You are the only hope."

"You are." She forces more of her blood down my throat and then rolls me on my side. There is a sharp pain in my back as she pulls out Ory's dagger. I still feel the poison in my system, however, crawling through my veins and feeding on my internal organs. Kalika opens the vein on her wrist and forces me to feed, and it is as if the current of her life energy overwhelms the poison, and I feel it die inside me. A peaceful warmth steals over my physical form. Already I think the wound in my throat has closed. Yet inside I am still in torment. Even as I sit up Kalika seems to lose strength and lies back down. The massive wound to her chest is still open and I cringe because I worry I may actually see her heart beating, or slowing down. I don't know, of course. I do try to open my vein to drip my blood over her wound, but she stops me.

"It's too late," she says.

This death I cannot bear.

"No," I moan.

"You see I did not want to harm the child. I just wanted to protect him from the Setians."

"That's why you came into this world?"

"Yes." She raises her left hand and touches my hair. "And to be your daughter."

The tears on my face are so red. They will stain my skin, I think, and I will carry the burden of this loss the rest of my days, out where people can see it. I want to bury my face in her chest but I am afraid I will hurt her more. So I take the hand she touches me with and I kiss it.

"I should have listened to you," I say.

"Yes."

"You never hurt the police, did you?"

"No."

"And you knew Eric had a fatal illness?"

"Yes. His suffering would have been worse if I had not killed him."

My voice is choked. "You should have told me."

This amuses her. "You hear what you wish. You are more human than you know. But that is your greatest strength as well. Krishna loves all humanity as his children."

"Who is the child, Kalika? Is he Krishna? Is he Christ?"

Her voice is weak, her gaze far away. "He is like me, the essence of all things. A name, a title, does not describe him. Divisions are for men. God knows only one being."

"Does the child need my help to survive?"

She is a long time answering. Her eyes are focused on the ceiling.

"You will help him. That is why you were born."

Sobs rack my body. "All this time you never lied to me."

That makes her look at me. "Once I did. When I told you I would not let you stand in my way to the child." A spasm shakes her body and I hear her heart skip as she begins to die. "I could never hurt you, Sita."

"How do I stop Ory?"

"Your age-old weapons, strength and cunning, will not do it."

"But what will?"

"Faith is stronger than stone," she whispers.

"The scripture." I am confused. "But it spoke against you."

That makes her smile. "Parts Suzama wrote. Parts Ory wrote to make it look like Suzama's writing."

"The papyrus about you was of a different texture."

"Yes. You cannot believe everything you read,

even when it is supposed to be scripture." A convulsion suddenly grips her body and her back arches off the floor. My tears are a river. Five thousand years of life and death have not prepared me for this. To see my own daughter die, all because of me—how cruel the irony is. Yet Kalika, with her failing strength, pulls my hand down and kisses my fingers. "Words cannot inspire faith. Only love can destroy the maya."

"Is this just an illusion to you? Even your own death?"

She squeezes my hand and her eyes are bright.

"You are no illusion. I really am your daughter." A sigh escapes her lips and her eyes close. Inside her chest I hear her heart stop, but there is air left in her lungs, and she says in that special soft voice of hers, "I love you, Mother."

Those are her last words.

She is gone, back to the abyss from which she came.

Another death, another farewell, waits for me on the shore, on the beach beneath Paula's house. There I find Dr. Seter slumped against a stone wall, his skin the blue color of a failing cardiac patient's. Seymour and Paula are nowhere to be seen. Dr. Seter has had a major heart attack and I do not have to stretch my imagination to figure out how he got it. James returned with the child and revealed that he was not a nice and kind son, after all. As I kneel beside the doctor, he opens his eyes and gasps for air.

"You're bleeding," he says.

I am soaked with blood but I am no longer bleeding.

"I am all right." I put a hand on his chest and feel his erratic pulse. "Can I get you a doctor?" I know that will not help him, and am relieved when he shakes his head.

"I am finished," he says, and his face is so sad. "I never knew."

"I didn't either."

He is bitter. "Suzama lied to us both."

"No. Most of the scripture was true. James only created the part that dealt with Kalika." I pause. "She was my daughter."

He is amazed. "Where is she now?"

"On the island. She's dead." I sigh. "We were fools."

He weeps for my pain. "I was the fool. It was my arrogance that made me believe God was giving me visions. That I understood the mind of God." He coughs. "James put those dreams in my mind. He led me to the scripture."

I nod. "He led you to where he buried it."

"But why would he do these things? How could he do them?"

"He was never your son. He only came into your life to use you. He possesses the body of the young man we see. He is neither young nor is he human. Please do not blame yourself, Dr. Seter. I fought with this creature long ago and I did not recognize him. If anyone is to blame it is I."

He stares up at me. "Who are you, Alisa?"

"I am your friend." I hug him. "And I will get the child back."

My words seem to comfort him. He dies a minute later but there is peace written on his face. He was a good man, I know.

Paula stands behind me.

"Sita," she says gently.

I turn and look at her. Around her neck she wears a blue scarf with gold threads running through it. These threads make a wonderful design, but I am in too much of hurry to pay it much heed. Letting go of Dr. Seter, I stand and step to her side.

"I know where the enemy is taking your child," I say.

She nods. She believes me, she always has. Such faith.

"Your friend," she says.

I grab her arms. "Seymour!"

She nods her head to the side. "He is out front. He has been shot."

"Is he dead?" I ask.

She hesitates. "He is close."

I gaze at the small island in the center of Emerald Bay. I had swum back ashore. It had not been easy to leave my daughter's body.

"Find a boat," I say to Paula. "That was my daughter who took your child, but she was only trying to protect him. Her body is on the island, in the house. Please bring her back here and wrap her in a blanket until I return." I turn away. "I will take care of Seymour."

She stops me. "I will help you with your friend first."

I shake my head. "No, Paula. I have to be alone with him to help him."

There are tears in her eyes. "Your daughter gave her life to save John?"

"Yes. She gave more than any of us knew."

Seymour lies on his side in a pool of blood fifty yards up the hill from Paula's house, wedged cruelly between two large rocks. James had shot him in the stomach. One close-range blast was enough. He is unconscious and slipping away fast. The child is gone, and this time I do not have the mystery and magic of the universe in a convenient vial in my pocket. The only way I can save him is to grant his oldest wish. That I will do for him because I love him, and I know Krishna will forgive me. Indeed, if I can only find the child again, and give him a chance to grow old enough to understand me, then I can ask him to take away my vow. Leaning over, I open a vein and whisper in Seymour's ear.

"Now, old buddy, just because you're going to be a vampire doesn't mean you automatically get to sleep with me. We'll have to date first."

I give him my blood. It is all I have to give.

18 ~

The next evening, at sunset, I arrive at the bluff in the desert where the child was conceived. The tall Joshua trees stand around me like guards that would offer me help if they could. But there is no one to help me. Even my own strength and cunning cannot aid me if I am to believe my daughter and Suzama.

I have brought the dagger James stuck into me. It is my only weapon, pitiful as it is.

Faith is stronger than stone.

James will not simply murder the child. The divine blood is as important to a demon as it is to a saint. Only the two do not make the same use of it. I know he will have to bring the child to this spot.

He did not locate the Suzama Center in Palm Springs, so close to this place, by coincidence. Plus my old friend has said as much.

Then the place of sanctity will be defiled by red stars, and only the innocent will see the blue light of heaven.

Am I the innocent? At the moment I feel far from it. I know Kalika told me that my thoughts blinded me but I still cannot stop thinking how she let James get so close to the child when she clearly knew what he was and where he was. Of course it could be argued that I stopped her from fleeing, yet in the last minutes of her mysterious life she was content to quit running and sit and play with the child to let what was to be be. James clearly used me to defeat Kalika; he could not have done it alone. Yet Kalika let herself be defeated. Was it because she wished to fulfill the ancient prophecy?

There the dark forces will once again converge on him, but a powerful angel of mistaken color will rescue him only to lose him again.

No one mistook Kalika more than her own mother.

But what am I to do now?

The rest is a mystery.

For once, I wish Suzama had hinted a little more.

What am I to have faith in? I do not miss the fact that Suzama placed faith and stone together in the same sentence, since it was Ory's control of the earth element that allowed him to defeat me the last time. All right, I have faith in the child. He seems like a cute little guy with incredible vibes and a darling smile. I love him, I really do, and I only got to hold him for a short time. But what am I supposed to do with this faith? It seems I should be able to use it somehow.

The sun slowly sets. The stars come out.

The moon has yet to rise.

I stare at the stars and pray for them to help me.

Then I realize something quite extraordinary.

The last time I went to see Suzama, she was wearing a blue scarf that had gold threads woven in it depicting the constellations in the sky, both the northern and the southern sky. Last night Paula was wearing a blue scarf as well, also woven with a pattern in gold thread. In fact, the more I think about it, the more convinced I am that the scarves are identical.

I am hardly given a chance to wonder how that could be possible.

Because something strange starts to happen.

The more I visualize those hauntingly beautiful star patterns in Suzama's scarf the brighter the stars above me grow. And what is even stranger is that this experience has already been described to me by Paula.

"The sky was filled with a million stars. They were so bright! I could have been in outer space. . . . It was almost as if I had been transported to another world, inside a huge star cluster, and was looking up at its nighttime sky."

The stars grow so bright I can feel their energy on the top of my head, streaming down into my whole body. One star in particular, a bright blue one straight overhead, seems to soar in brilliance as I look up and concentrate on it. It grows in size. It could be a blue saucer racing toward the earth. A high-pitched sound starts to vibrate through the area. Paula's words are still in my mind.

"The rays of the star pierced my eyelids. The sound pierced my ears. I wanted to scream. Maybe I was screaming. But I don't think I was in actual physical pain. It was more as if I was being transformed."

I think I am screaming too. This is how it felt when the moon would pour into the top of my head and turn me into a nice friendly ghost that could float off on the desert wind. But this vibration is thousands of times more intense. It feels as if the starlight is irradiating the nerve fibers in my spinal cord, changing them into magnetic circuits on a cosmic grid, a stellar system of communication and propulsion that has been there since the beginning of time, even though no one imagined it existed. I only have to want to plug into it to be able to use it. At the same time, I don't know if I am in physical distress. Blissful terror is a better expression for it; the entire experience is destroying everything that I thought is me, and yet there is relief in the destruction as well. But just when I think I will either explode or turn into a galactic android, it stops.

Unlike Paula I do not black out.

I am suddenly floating high above the desert.

In a glistening blue body.

It is very nice. This body, this state of being, carries none of the burdens of the physical realm. I am quite content just to float around with the stars. I can still see the desert far below, the rolling hills of sand, the edges of the shadows of the tall Joshuas shimmering under the intoxicating rays of the galaxy's stars. I realize then how crucial a role the stars play in our lives, their constant subtle influence bubbles on the edges of energy fields we are unaware we possess. Yet I do not think about it too much because I cannot be bothered thinking.

After some time I become aware that there is a highly dense bundle of red energy descending from above. Just the sight of it fills me with revulsion and I want to get out of its way. It is the opposite of what I am; it is neither love nor bliss. I desire to avoid it at all costs and I know that I merely have to will myself to be gone.

It is only then that I fully remember who I am.

The transformation had caused me momentary amnesia.

I remember why I have come to the desert. The child.

Far below me, I see James holding the baby. He is encapsulated in the same red light, but the baby glows in his arms like a tiny blue star. My awareness goes up and down, back and forth between them. As the red energy bundle comes closer I see that it is taking on substance, gaining the vague shape of a flying saucer. It seems as if from an unseen realm I am presented with a choice. I can try to enter this ship, in my blue body, and stop what is being planned by the Setians, or I can simply float away and be happy. Yet if I choose the former course, there is danger. I can become trapped, I sense. My very soul can be chained in a place of demons.

Because if I go into the ship I will have to go into a demon.

The choice, the universe seems to say, is mine.

I think of Kalika then, of her great sacrifice.

This thought makes the choice for me.

I float into the ship.

It is a vessel of serpents. There are six of them, big ugly brutes with long tails and scaly hides, thick snouts and cold, dead eyes, all sitting around a square viewing port and each manipulating controls of some kind. But one is clearly in charge. Besides being the largest, he has the most highly charged energy field. He is like a swollen red sun from the wrong side of the galaxy. And I know he is the one I have to attack.

In a moment I am inside his body.

His mind. What a pit it is.

This is a true Setian, a genuine demon. His lusts and passions seem to spin in a vortex, yet he is highly intelligent and has worked long and hard to attain the rank he now holds. He is being sent by his superiors on this important mission to bring back the human avatar, the crowning jewel of all prizes. If he is successful, he will be given an opportunity to consume the energy of the child with his masters. His name is Croka and he lives off the emotions of hate and fear. They are food to him as humans are food to him. He can consume the holy child and be strengthened by him. On his home world, I see that black ceremonies will be performed to prepare the feast.

But Croka is not yet aware that I am in his mind.

The ship lands in the desert and the six Setians climb out into the night air. Still inside Croka I move with them. Yet I know this ship, these creatures even, are not really physical. The average human, if he or she were to pass this spot, would see nothing, yet he or she would most certainly feel a great dread. Simply to be inside Croka's mind is a torture as great as any that I have ever known. It is as bad as seeing my own daughter die. Yet I am now determined that her death will not be in vain.

James can see the Setians. He bows as they sit in a semicircle around him. He stands respectfully, the child in his hands. Little John gazes at them in wonder, the red light cracking and sparking around his blue aura. Clearly the baby can see them, yet he does not cry out. The reptilian Setians are large; even though they are sitting, their ugly heads rise above James's. The one farthest from Croka bids James bring the child closer. It seems the monster wants to gloat over it, paw it even, and this to me is unbearable. Yet I know the creature will not really harm it. The feast is planned for later, on the Setian hell planet.

James brings the child to each beast, and each one pokes at it a bit. The child does not cry out and this seems to annoy both the visitors and James. Finally it is brought to Croka, but before he can touch it my eyes fasten on the child's eyes, and so, in effect, the Setian commander's eyes are also focused, against his will actually, on the same spot, on the profound gaze of the infant. It is only then that Croka becomes aware that I am sitting deep within his mind, and I understand that this is the moment of greatest danger. For Croka, like most advanced Setians, is a master of *seedling,* the manipulation of will, and I feel his furious will suddenly rise up against mine.

He reaches for me too late, because I already have the *kavach* of the child's gaze, the armor or protection of the avatar, and seedling loses all power in the presence of a saint. Like Ory of old, Croka carries a dagger in his silver belt, and I reach for it with Croka's own arm. Before the Setian can stop me, before James even knows what I am up to, I stab the blade in James's left eye.

Then all at once I am back in my vampiric body.

Back in the desert with only James and the child standing before me. The saucer and the Setians appear to be gone. But James is in pain, and I realize that I have already stabbed his *own* knife into his eye. Well, I think, this time I must have come out of nowhere on him. Quickly, before he can recover, I withdraw the knife and poke it in his other eye, effectively blinding him. He howls in pain and the blood that pours from his wounds is black and foul smelling.

He drops the child and puts his hands over his torn eyes.

I catch the child before he hits the ground and set him down gently.

Then I turn back to James.

"Jimmy," I say sweetly, "where do you want me to put the poison? It is a new and improved brand. Guaranteed to kill even a slimy lizard like you."

He swings at me with his right arm and misses, spinning helplessly in front of me, and I stab the knife in his spine behind his heart, just where he shot my daughter. Screaming in agony, he falls to his knees and bows his head. His flaying hands desperately strain to pull out the knife but I know just how powerful the poison is, soaked deep in the folds of the blade itself. He is already doomed.

"Sita," he gasps. "You don't understand what this moment means to this part of the galaxy. You can't interfere."

I laugh. "Are you talking about your lizard friends? They are probably still here right now. I'm sure they are, but they don't have a physical body like mine. They have to work through scummy agents like you. And right now their poor agent can't even see well enough to tie his own shoes. Oh my."

His face is a mass of black blood. Yet it is as if he is weeping.

"You can't do this," he says. "This night was planned for ages."

I kick him and he cries out again.

"Yeah?" I say. "Who planned tonight for ages? Not Suzama. Not me. I just wish there were a swarm of flies here and I had the luxury of killing you slowly. But I have other things to do right now." I grab him by his mane of messy hair and pull his head back, exposing his throat. "This, I am going to enjoy."

"Wait!" he cries. "I have not completed my mission! I will not be allowed to transfer to another body!"

I pull out the dagger impaled in his spine.

"James," I say. "I honestly don't care."

"Stop!" he screams. "I don't want to die!"

Ah, there is a divine sweetness to total revenge. God might not agree but I would argue the point.

"Then you should never have been born," I say.

His blood, when I open his neck, flows like black ink.

There is a loud hiss in my ear. The wind tugs at my hair.

A flash of red light momentarily blurs the stars. The Setians have left, and in a hurry.

I let go of James and he falls dead on the sand.

Drawing in a deep breath of fresh air, I laugh out loud.

The child laughs with me as I carry him back to the road.

I think he likes me. Really, he is so cute.

Look for Christopher Pike's

The Last Vampire 6
CREATURES OF FOREVER

Coming mid-August 1996

About the Author

CHRISTOPHER PIKE was born in Brooklyn, New York, but grew up in Los Angeles, where he lives to this day. Prior to becoming a writer, he worked in a factory, painted houses, and programmed computers. His hobbies include astronomy, meditating, running, playing with his nieces and nephews, and making sure his books are prominently displayed in local bookstores. He is the author of *Last Act, Spellbound, Gimme a Kiss, Remember Me, Scavenger Hunt, Final Friends* 1, 2, and 3, *Fall into Darkness, See You Later, Witch, Die Softly, Bury Me Deep, Whisper of Death, Chain Letter 2: The Ancient Evil, Master of Murder, Monster, Road to Nowhere, The Eternal Enemy, The Immortal, The Wicked Heart, The Midnight Club, The Last Vampire, The Last Vampire 2: Black Blood, The Last Vampire 3: Red Dice, Remember Me 2: The Return, Remember Me 3: The Last Story, The Lost Mind, The Visitor, The Starlight Crystal,* and *The Last Vampire 4: Phantom,* all available from Archway Paperbacks. *Slumber Party, Weekend, Chain Letter,* and *Sati*—an adult novel about a very unusual lady—are also by Mr. Pike.